Readers love the Stories by ANDRE

A Shared Range

"*Shared Range* is a love story at heart with lots of action and content to keep any reader interested."

—MM Good Book Reviews

A Troubled Range

"Andrew Grey has another winner with his follow up Range story, and I, for one, want to know when he will be back to the wilds of Wyoming again."

—Love Romances & More

An Unsettled Range

"Andrew Grey brings a multitude of issues into his story… All outstanding elements, all beautifully folded into a heartwarming story."

—Scattered Thoughts and Rogue Words

A Foreign Range

"Mr. Grey is the master at building sexual tension between his characters, but there is always the emotional attachment as well…"

—Guilty Indulgence

An Isolated Range

"I can honestly say that this is one author that whenever he has a release, I need to get it immediately."

—Dawn's Reading Nook

A Volatile Range

"May be my favorite in a series that I have enjoyed very much."

—Mrs. Condit & Friends Read Books

By ANDREW GREY

Accompanied by a Waltz
Copping a Sweetest Day Feel
Crossing Divides
Cruise for Christmas
Dominant Chord
Dutch Treat
A Heart Without Borders
In Search of a Story
A Lion in Tails
Mariah the Christmas Moose
North to the Future
One Good Deed
A Present in Swaddling Clothes
Shared Revelations
Simple Gifts
Snowbound in Nowhere
Stranded • Taken
Three Fates (Anthology)
To Have, Hold, and Let Go
Whipped Cream
Work Me Out (Anthology)

ART SERIES
Legal Artistry • Artistic Appeal • Artistic Pursuits • Legal Tender

BOTTLED UP STORIES
The Best Revenge • Bottled Up • Uncorked • An Unexpected Vintage

BRONCO'S BOYS
Inside Out • Upside Down

THE BULLRIDERS
A Wild Ride • A Daring Ride • A Courageous Ride

BY FIRE SERIES
Redemption by Fire • Strengthened by Fire • Burnished by Fire • Heat Under Fire

CHEMISTRY SERIES
Organic Chemistry • Biochemistry • Electrochemistry

Published by DREAMSPINNER PRESS
http://www.dreamspinnerpress.com

By ANDREW GREY (continued)

GOOD FIGHT SERIES
The Good Fight • The Fight Within • The Fight for Identity • Takoda and Horse

LOVE MEANS… SERIES
Love Means… No Shame • Love Means… Courage
Love Means… No Boundaries
Love Means… Freedom • Love Means … No Fear
Love Means… Healing
Love Means… Family • Love Means… Renewal • Love Means… No Limits
Love Means… Patience

SENSES STORIES
Love Comes Silently • Love Comes in Darkness
Love Comes Home • Love Comes Around

SEVEN DAYS STORIES
Seven Days • Unconditional Love

STORIES FROM THE RANGE
A Shared Range • A Troubled Range • An Unsettled Range
A Foreign Range • An Isolated Range • A Volatile Range • A Chaotic Range

TALES FROM KANSAS
Dumped in Oz • Stuck in Oz • Trapped in Oz

TASTE OF LOVE STORIES
A Taste of Love • A Serving of Love • A Helping of Love
A Slice of Love

WORK OUT SERIES
Spot Me • Pump Me Up • Core Training • Crunch Time
Positive Resistance • Personal Training • Cardio Conditioning

Published by DREAMSPINNER PRESS
http://www.dreamspinnerpress.com

A Chaotic RANGE

ANDREW GREY

Dreamspinner Press

Published by
DREAMSPINNER PRESS

5032 Capital Circle SW, Suite 2, PMB# 279, Tallahassee, FL 32305-7886 USA
http://www.dreamspinnerpress.com/

A Chaotic Range
© 2014 Andrew Grey.

Cover Art
© 2014 Reese Dante.
www.reesedante.com
Cover content is for illustrative purposes only and any person depicted on the cover is a model.

ISBN: 978-1-63216-022-5
Digital ISBN: 978-1-63216-150-5
Library of Congress Control Number: 2014945936
First Edition November 2014

Printed in the United States of America
∞
This paper meets the requirements of
ANSI/NISO Z39.48-1992 (Permanence of Paper).

To Dominic. My stability in a chaotic world.

Chapter One

SNOW BLEW in front of, behind, and all around the red car, so thick the hood looked white now. Every few seconds, Brian was able to see something on the side of the road. He'd passed a town a ways back and wished he'd stopped. He had been looking for a place to turn around for the past twenty minutes, but he'd found nowhere wider than his car. The needle on the gas gauge took another lurch toward empty, and Brian realized he didn't have much time left. He had to find a place somewhere, somehow, but he saw nothing but white. Occasionally, he saw a fence post by the side of the road—the only indication that he was actually still on the road. His heart pounded louder and louder. Thankfully, the heater continued to pour out warm air, but that was the only saving grace right now.

Something green stuck out of the snow on the side of the road. Brian pulled to a stop and leaned over to that side of the car. A road sign and another, homemade sign with an arrow pointed down the other street, where he could just make out tire tracks. He took that as an indication that there had to be someone down that way. He made the turn, and the wind changed. It was coming from behind him now and he could see a little farther ahead of him, but no farther to the side. He kept going and going, hoping to see some sign of life, but the tracks petered out and he had to blaze a trail through drifting snow. Brian knew if he didn't find something soon, he would be totally out of luck.

The wind died down and the view in front of the car opened up. He could see the land in front of him: a few trees and some white mounds off to the left. He hoped like hell those were buildings. Then, just like that, the wind roared back, the opening closed, and visibility got even worse. Brian was barely moving, and the sound under the tires changed as the ride roughened. Brian realized he was off the road and turned the wheel, but he overcompensated. Before he could turn the wheel back, the car started fishtailing back and forth and then spun, and for a few seconds he was going backward. Then the back of the car dropped and came to an abrupt halt, jarring him back and then forward. Thankfully, his seat belt kept him from hitting the wheel or the window, but he was definitely whipped a little.

"Shit!" Brian breathed and blinked a few times, taking stock to ensure he wasn't hurt. The engine had cut out. He tried to start it again, but though the engine turned over, it just wouldn't start. He was most likely too low on gas. Brian stared out the windshield for a few minutes in a daze and then became fully aware of himself once again. He unfastened his seat belt and tried to open his door. It didn't budge, and he pushed harder, but the snow must have been packed around it because it barely moved at all. The wind, however, found the crack and began pushing its way inside. Brian yanked the door closed. He turned on the fan to force what heat he could get from the engine into the car and then turned it off. He left the hazard lights on, hoping someone might pass or see them if there was a break in the wind. Brian knew it wasn't likely. He felt the heat slowly dissipate as he sat.

After a few minutes, he figured he had nothing to lose. The car was getting colder and colder, so he shifted to the passenger seat and tried that door. It was worse and would only open an inch no matter how hard he pushed. Brian was stuck, he knew it, and there wasn't a damned thing he could do about it. As it got colder, he decided to try his door again. By rocking it back and forth, Brian was able to get it open about six inches, but he'd robbed the last remaining heat from inside the car to do it. He continued working and managed to get the door to open just enough that he could get out.

Brian stepped into snow that went up well past his knees. The car had plowed into a snowbank that had been built up from past efforts to plow the road, with light snow on top of heavy. The back wheels of the car were away from the road, with the body and front of the car resting on the mound. He wasn't going anywhere, not without help, and all he could see in every direction was white. Nothing but white. He remembered briefly seeing what might have been buildings during the break in the wind, but he wasn't sure if he'd passed them already or not. His best bet was to get back in the car, try to keep warm, and hope the wind and storm died down soon so someone would see him. So he got back in the car and pulled the door closed. As soon as the door clicked shut, he wished he'd tried to get to his things in the trunk. He reached for the release and it opened, so he got back out and struggled to make his way around to the back.

He managed to open the trunk and somehow keep it open against the wind and snow as he grabbed his duffel and a small backpack. Then he tried to climb back into the car. He slung the backpack over a shoulder and used his free hand to pull himself along the car to the door. He grasped it and managed to leverage himself around the door. He pushed the bags through the opening and then squeezed inside, yanking the door closed with what sounded like a thud of finality. He wasn't going out again until something changed.

Brian's hands ached and his ears and face felt as though they were frozen. He tried the engine again, and it blessedly turned over and started. "Thank God," he whispered and placed his hands over the vents blasting heat into the space. They tingled along with his ears and face as his skin warmed.

After five minutes he was warm and had stopped shivering. He'd reached for the keys to shut down the engine when it sputtered and then went silent. The only source of heat other than himself was gone. Brian listened to the wind as it howled and raged outside the car. There wasn't a damn thing he could do. He pulled open his duffel bag and shrugged off his coat. He was wearing a sweatshirt, but he found another and pulled it over his head. Then he put his coat back on. The jeans he'd been wearing were wet because the snow he'd picked up outside had melted in the heat, so he shucked them off, along with his wet shoes, and threw them on the passenger-side floor. He had a pair of sweatpants somewhere, so he rummaged for them quickly because he was starting to shiver again in nothing but his underwear. He pulled on the sweats and then a pair of jeans. He had to get creative, but at least the weight he'd lost in the last few weeks made room inside the jeans for the sweats.

Brian stripped off his socks, then found two fresh pairs and pulled those on. He smacked his forehead. He had left his boots in the trunk. He didn't dare risk getting his last dry clothes wet now, and he couldn't face another trip out of the car. He'd just have to work with what he had. He found a hat in the duffel and pulled it on, wishing he'd had it earlier. Then he rummaged for something to put on his hands. He couldn't find anything and figured he could just shove his hands in his pockets. Then he climbed in the backseat and pulled out the few remaining clothes he had left. In the bottom of the duffel he found a bath towel. He wrapped that around his feet and curled up on the seat with the rest of his clothes like a makeshift patchwork quilt on top of him, resting his head where the seat and back passenger door met.

Other than the wind and his own breathing, the world was silent. Brian lost track of time with only his thoughts to mark its passing. He'd screwed up shit in his life so bad. This was not how he'd pictured his life ending, waiting as cold slowly made its way through the clothing that surrounded him. He worked his hands out of the sleeves of his coat and hugged them to his body. It was a decent coat, but not nearly warm enough for this kind of weather.

The car windows fogged and then formed ice crystals on the inside as the moisture from his breath began to freeze. He'd had such plans for his life. His parents didn't know shit about anything, and he'd left to make his fortune. He was going to be famous in rodeo. That would show them. His hometown of Casper would throw him a parade when he came to town. Well, that hadn't happened. He knew now it couldn't have, no matter what, but he'd been a kid full of delusions of grandeur that the world had slowly pulled away from him. Nothing he planned seemed to happen. He wasn't talented enough for rodeo, and all he really knew was ranch work, but that didn't seem to be working out either.

Brian closed his eyes and let the movie of his life play. There was nothing else to do, so he figured he might as well wallow in the screwed-up mess his life had become. He'd had his last ranch job near Cheyenne the longest of any of them. He'd really liked the place too. The owners had been good people and they'd treated him decently, even after they found out about the "liking broncs instead of fillies" thing. But the other hands had been a completely different matter. The news had spread like wildfire, and after that, nothing had gone right. The guys had made sure of that, and then, well, he'd had to leave—in the middle of a harsh winter when no ranch on earth was hiring anybody for anything. His only chance was to find a job somewhere and hope that spring would bring something better. Look at him: thirty-two years old, out of work, crouched in the back of his car trying to stay alive, not really sure he cared if someone rescued him. Maybe it was like his old man had said— he'd have been better off if he'd just curled up somewhere and died. Maybe his father had been prophetic. He certainly had crawled here, and unless someone came along, it looked like he would very well die here.

He tried to see out, but the windows were fully frozen now, and they appeared to have already been covered in snow. Hell, for all he knew, the entire car had been covered in snow and someone could pass right by and never realize he was there.

Brian closed his eyes and willed time to pass faster. If he was going to die, he might as well get it over with. He was thirsty now and growing more so by the minute. His stomach rumbled and gurgled incessantly, telling him it was empty, a condition he'd become accustomed to more and more lately. No, there was nothing to do but wait for whatever was going to happen. Let it come.

Brian tried not to move too much. His body had warmed up the seat where he was lying. The rest of the car was cold as hell. He'd completely lost track of time. One thing he had noticed was that the soft beeping of the hazard lights had stopped. The battery was dead now, and it wasn't likely anyone would find him. He debated getting out of the car and making a last-ditch effort to find help. But the howling wind reminded him of what waited, and he knew that was worse. They always said to stay in the car. Even as cold as it was, the car was warmer than the wind. That he knew, so he stayed put.

His blanket of clothes began to chill, and he felt the cold begin to seep through his clothing. It started with his feet and legs and worked upward. His feet began to tingle and then ache. He wriggled his toes and rubbed his legs and feet together before pulling them up as close to his body as he could. He also shifted some more of the covering over them, and that seemed to help, but it was only temporary. "So this is how the end starts," Brian whispered aloud, hoping that if this was the end, it happened fast.

The slow chill continued. He thought back to when he was a kid and said one of the prayers he'd learned a long time ago and hadn't thought about for years. Then he closed his eyes and waited for the end to come.

Cold washed over him, and the shivering that had started earlier increased.

"David, Phillip, there's someone in here," a masculine voice called.

Brian was scared to open his eyes, wondering if he was imagining things. The car door near his feet opened, cold whipped around him, and Brian shook more. He opened his eyes and saw what looked like an abominable snowman moving around in the doorway.

"Bring the blankets from behind the seat. It doesn't matter if they're for horses, we need them now."

Brian opened his mouth, but all that happened was his teeth chattered.

"You're going to be all right now," the man said. Brian didn't know how much longer he would be able to take this cold, and he closed his eyes, shivering uncontrollably.

A weight settled over him, blocking out the wind and cold. It smelled like horse, but he didn't care. He felt another weight settle, blocking what little light there had been, but also cutting the wind. A hand reached under the blanket, and Brian realized the guy was pulling out his makeshift covers. "Here, take this back to the truck."

"How are we going to get him out of there, Haven?" another male voice asked.

"David and I are going to carry him. Take his bags and put them in the truck, along with his shoes." Brian heard the guy shifting around in the car. "We need to work fast. See if there's anything else in there while I get him wrapped up. We have to get him warm."

He heard digging and then the passenger side door opened, turning the car into a wind tunnel. "David, help me move him this way."

Someone took his feet and pulled him along the seat toward the door. "Come on around here." The passenger car door closed, and all Brian could do was keep his eyes shut and let them do whatever they wanted with him. He was in no position to stop anyone.

"Okay, I have you," the man said. "Can you stand at all?"

Brian nodded and did his best to balance in the doorway of the car. The wind came right at him and threatened to blow him back, but before it could, the man heaved him over his shoulder and began moving. All Brian saw was the back of legs, coattail, and snow.

Then the wind stopped and warmth, real warmth, surrounded him. A door closed, and everything went quiet except the sound of an engine and a fan blowing heat. He continued shivering, but it slowly abated. His legs began to tingle and then ache. His feet did the same thing, and then finally his toes. He wasn't going to freeze to death after all.

The truck door opened, and Brian did his best to sit up. The other guys climbed inside and squeezed next to him. It was a tight fit, but he didn't care. He'd been found and was warm. That was all that mattered at the moment. "Who are you?"

"It's all right. We have you now," the more familiar voice said. "The storm is beginning to move on. David saw something red in the snow—your car. Thank goodness we got to you."

Brian nodded and stared out the window as they began to move.

They didn't travel long before turning into a drive. A low ranch house appeared ahead of them, with other buildings and barns along the side. So he had seen something—it hadn't been his imagination. "Thank you," Brian sighed.

"You're lucky David here is an eagle-eye. No one else spotted you," the man who seemed to be in charge said. Brian looked at David and squinted slightly. He looked familiar, but Brian couldn't figure out where he knew him from. "We're going to get you inside and we'll figure everything out. Do you think you can walk?"

"Yeah," Brian said. The feeling in his feet and legs had come back and they ached slightly, but the majority of the pain was gone.

"Phillip, hon, could you please get his shoes for him? I think they got shoved back there with everything else." The truck pulled to a stop, and the driver left the truck running. Two of the men got out, and one of them handed Brian his shoes.

"I'll get him inside, Haven," Phillip said to the driver. "Go ahead and take care of what needs to be done."

"Thanks," Haven said and then patted Brian's arm. "And call Dakota to see if he can make it over here to check him out as soon as the roads are passable." Brian turned and watched the man—Haven—fiddle with his phone. "Guys, it looks like we got about an hour, no more, before another band of this crap hits. Let's get feed out to the herds, as much as we can."

"I'm Phillip, and this is David," the slim man said to Brian. "Hold on to your shoes, and I'll help you in the house, where it's good and warm, and get something hot in you." The man turned to David. "Go on and help Haven. If he's only got an hour, he'll need everyone. I'll see to…."

"Brian."

"Brian, here. No problem."

"You sure?" David asked.

"Yeah. Go. If we start losing cattle, there will be hell to pay for all of us," Phillip said. "And tell all the men I'll put a huge pot of soup on the stove in the house. They're to come on in once they're done."

David hurried away. Brian shrugged off the blankets. He managed to get his shoes on, but gave up on tying them. His fingers weren't nimble enough to do that.

"Come on. Let's get you settled and warm," Phillip said.

Brian slid out of the truck, and Phillip put one of the blankets over his shoulders. Brian walked toward the house, and Phillip held the door so he could get inside. Phillip fussed around him and then took the blanket away once they were in the house. Brian stood and looked around the room, waiting to be told what to do.

"Have a seat here," Phillip said, patting the back of one of the large chairs. Brian did as he was told and sank into the comfortable chair. Phillip hurried away and then returned with a different blanket. Brian took off his coat and wet shoes, and Phillip draped the soft blanket over him.

"I'm going to get your stuff," Phillip said. "Just stay here. I'll be right back, and then I can see about some food." He left Brian alone, and Brian looked around the room. This was obviously a prosperous place. The furniture was nice, and the floors were gleaming stone tile that extended as far as he could see. The décor was that of a ranch, masculine, but with touches of flair and class. The endearment Haven had used in reference to Phillip hadn't gone unnoticed. At least maybe these people wouldn't be running him off because of the gay thing. They might because of the other stuff, but probably not *that*.

Brian got comfortable, and Phillip came back inside a few minutes later. "I'm gonna take this down to the guest room." He lifted the duffel and wrinkled his nose. "No, I'm going to wash all this first." Phillip zoomed away, and Brian wondered if Phillip had any speed other than fast forward. He paid little attention to anything other than the fact that he was warm. When Phillip returned, he brought Brian a plate with cheese and crackers and a mug of what smelled like cocoa. "It's instant, but it should warm you for now."

"Thank you," Brian said quietly.

"You're welcome. I'm going to start some lunch because I know you're hungry from the yelling your stomach keeps doing, and the men will be cold clear through by the time they're done feeding the cattle. Once I've got things going, you can tell me what you were doing out there on a day like this." Phillip flashed him a warm smile that under different circumstances might have given Brian ideas. But judging from the gold band on Phillip's left hand, he was clearly spoken for. And Brian had already made that mistake one too many times. Nope, he was swearing off guys, period. Didn't matter if he thought they were interested. He'd gotten into trouble more than once getting busy with cowboys and guys he worked with. Oh, they were happy as hell when he was sucking their cocks or letting them fuck him, but the rest of the time it was tits this and ass that. And most definitely not the kind he was interested in.

The door opened with a bang. "*Shit!*"

"Haven, what is it?" Phillip asked as he came in from the other room.

"Damn loader decided now would be a good time to take a crap. Mario's sending one of the guys over to take a look at it. Thank God he said they were done with the feeding on their end, so he's sending equipment and men, but of course it had to pick today to pull this crap." He stomped through the house, came back out with a huge thermos, and went straight outside. Brian picked up the plate from the coffee table and began to eat. As soon as the food hit his stomach, he realized he was ravenous. He drank the cocoa, which was a little grainy, but sweet and hot. It warmed him from the inside, and that and the cheese and crackers gave his belly something to do other than growl at him.

Brian watched out the window and listened to Phillip in the kitchen. It was still windy and snowing, but he could see almost out to the road now. He thought he could make out the red of his car by the side of the road if he looked just right. He could have died that close to help.

Rumbling started as vehicles pulled down the drive, a lot of them. Men got off, and the vibrations from heavy equipment rattled the house. The beep, beep, beep sounded as one of them backed up. Brian pushed the blanket away. With all the layers he was wearing, he was beginning to get warm. Thankfully, he was feeling better. "Is there something I can do to help?"

"No," Phillip called from the other room. "I got things going in here and I'll be right back in." Pots clanked and banged on the stove. Soon the heavenly scent of chicken soup filled the air. Brian swallowed and tried not to think about the last time he'd had a real homemade meal. Talk about a last supper. Brian sighed and waited for Phillip to come back in. He wasn't sure how much he should say about what had happened and where he'd been going. It would only make trouble for both him and them.

The snow seemed to have let up, and Brian stared outside as the yard emptied just as quickly as it had filled, every vehicle loaded with cattle feed. He hoped they were all careful, but then they probably knew every bump and slick spot in this area.

The house continued filling with the scent of food, and Brian's stomach rumbled again.

"Phillip," a man called as he pushed open the door.

"Dakota, I'll be right there," Phillip called, and he came into the living room as the man closed the door and began shedding cold winter gear. "This is Brian. Haven, David, and I rescued him from his car in the ditch, and he was nearly frozen. We got him warmed up, and I've given him a little something to eat."

"I'm Dakota, from up the road. I'm also a doctor, and I want to check you over for frostbite and make sure you're truly okay. How long were you in the car before they found you?"

Brian held out his hands, and Dakota looked them over. "I don't know. It could have been minutes or hours. I lost track of everything."

"What time do you think you went into the ditch?"

"Maybe nine or nine thirty, I guess."

"It's past noon now, so about three hours. As cold and windy as it was, you were very lucky." Dakota released his hands. "Can I look at your feet?" Brian shifted and took off his socks. His feet were still red. "Can you wiggle your toes?" He did, and Dakota looked at each one. "I'll repeat myself: you were really lucky. These look close to frostbite. We'll need to watch them for a few days to make sure all the circulation has come back. Keep them warm and moving. That's the best thing right now." Dakota went through the rest of an exam, listening to Brian's heart and lungs, then said, "You need to take it easy for a little while. That cold air got into your lungs good, so you need to give them a chance to recover as well."

Dakota began packing things up. "I have to go into town. With this weather, the hospital is swamped," he told Phillip. "Make sure Haven knows to call if he needs anything."

"I will," Phillip said. "Drive carefully."

"One of the plows is on its way to the house, and I'll ride in with them," Dakota said and then turned back to Brian. "I want to look at your feet again tomorrow." Dakota shared what Brian assumed was a meaningful glance with Phillip, because he nodded slowly. Phillip showed Dakota to the door once he'd dressed again and then stepped outside briefly with him.

"Dang," Phillip said when he came back in. "The wind and snow are picking up again." He went over to look out the window and then picked up the plate and cup and returned to the kitchen. He came back with a refill of the cocoa, handed the cup to Brian, and sat down. "I'll put you up in the guest room for tonight, but I need to know what you were doing out on those roads in a car like that on a day like this."

Brian opened his mouth, but Phillip cut him off.

"Before that, why don't you tell me your name?" Phillip said. He might have seemed a little rushed before, but when Phillip concentrated on him, his gaze was intense.

"Brian Applewright," he said. He'd thought about giving a false name, but figured it wouldn't do any good. He knew one of the men, David, from somewhere—he just couldn't put his finger on where. But if they knew each other, a lie wouldn't hold water. "I lost my job a few days ago at a ranch about forty miles south of here, and I was trying to find work, figure out what to do…. I don't know. I came through town and thought about stopping, but I had no money, so I kept going, and the weather got worse. I couldn't see crap and was looking for someplace to pull over when I spun out and ended up in your ditch."

Phillip nodded once and narrowed his gaze. "Why'd you get fired at this time of year? Everyone is hunkered down waiting for spring, keeping on as few guys as possible. You must have made the cut."

Brian knew he couldn't lie, but telling the whole truth wasn't something he was willing to do either. "I didn't get along with most of the guys when they found out…." God, it was hard just to say the words. "I'm gay."

"Ah," Phillip said.

"Yeah. The owners of the ranch were okay and it didn't matter to them, but they said my work was suffering. I got sabotaged by the other guys because they didn't want me around." Brian wasn't sure Phillip believed him at first, but he met Phillip's gaze without flinching. "I worked there for almost three years without an issue, but as soon as word got around, things started happening. Gates were left open that I was supposed to close when I knew I'd closed them, stuff like that." It was too much to hope that he could get a job here, but at least he had a warm place to stay for the night. "I was suddenly a bad worker, a problem, and a troublemaker all rolled into one. In the middle of winter, I was given my pay and told in the nicest way possible that I wasn't needed anymore."

Phillip sat back in his chair and shook his head. "People are dumb sometimes." He cradled his mug. "I'll tell you a story. I've known Dakota for quite a few years, and I came out here to visit him. When I did, I brought Wally along. Anyway, those two hit it off like nobody's business. Been happy as clams for years now. But when Wally first got here, some guys decided they didn't like him. Decided to teach the small guy a lesson. Dakota took out one, and by the time Wally was done, he had laid out two huge men—had them writhing in pain, standing over them telling them that if they moved, he'd shove their noses into their brains. After that, word got around fast. No one messes with Wally or his friends. See, Wally's a vet, and he helps just about everyone. Rescues lions and tigers. Keeps them in pens out back."

"You're kidding," Brian said. He wasn't sure where Phillip was going with this, but the story was engaging enough.

"Nope. Used to have one that liked to have his belly rubbed. Damn lion would roll on his back when he saw Wally. Looked like a huge lion carpet." Phillip chortled. "Guess I got off topic a little. The thing is, just because you're gay doesn't mean you have to take the crap folks want to dish out. Here on this ranch, we're good people. We help our neighbors and do right by folks. We don't discriminate against anyone. But we don't stand for any trouble, and the men all know about us."

"Us?"

"Yeah. Brian, it seems you stumbled into what has to be one of the gayest corners of Wyoming." Phillip settled back in his chair.

Who cared what the point of Phillip's story was? "Do you need some help? I've been around ranches most of my life. Grew up around Casper. Daddy was a foreman on a ranch before he died. I'm great with horses and I know cattle. I know a little about fixing most things, but I'm really good with leather and tack. The ranch I grew up on, the daughter rode rodeo, and I used to make all her bridles and things for shows. I don't have the tools any longer, but I could probably get some."

"Wait a minute," Phillip said, putting up his hands. "I don't make those decisions. Hiring is done by Haven and Dakota. I suggest, if you want a job, you talk to them when you see Dakota tomorrow."

"I thought Dakota lived on the next ranch," Brian asked, totally confused.

"We merged the two ranches a few years ago. Dakota is like the CEO, and Haven manages the day-to-day work. I do the books, and Wally takes care of the animals." The wind rattled the windows and Phillip got up, staring out. "Thank goodness," he said and left the room. The front door opened, and people began filing inside. "Take off your coats and stuff and put them in the laundry room," Phillip called from the kitchen. "I got soup on, so come sit at the table and we'll get you all warmed up."

The guys did as Phillip said, and Brian followed suit, joining the rest of the men around the table in the large ranch kitchen. He sat off to one side and listened while the men talked about the weather and stuff.

"Guys, this is Brian," Phillip said.

"He the guy they rescued from out of the car?" one of the men asked.

"Yes," David said from down the way.

Brian nodded to him. In that instant, it hit him. "Davey Newsome?" he asked as the pieces suddenly fell into place.

"Yeah," David said and leaned forward. "Oh God, I remember you. Brian Apple... something. The last name escapes me, but I remember. You were a year behind me." David turned to the guys. "Brian and I went to the same high school in Casper. Small world, isn't it?'

Brian nodded and turned away. He wondered if David was one of the gay people Phillip had talked about. Brian had had such a crush on him in high school. David had been an athlete—all the girls had followed him around, and the guys had wanted to be just like him. "Yeah. It's been a long time," he said quietly and turned away as Phillip began passing out bowls.

"Where's Haven?" Phillip asked.

"He said he'd be right in," the guy sitting next to Brian said. He was big and looked strong as an ox. "Name's Gus," he said, turning to Brian with a quick nod. Phillip put a plate of bread, some salad, cheese, crackers, raw vegetables, and dressings on the table before returning for more soup.

The guys began eating right away, so Brian did the same when his plate and bowl were placed in front of him.

Haven came in a little later and took the last empty place at the table. "We did good. The cattle have food and they'll be able to keep warm."

"The group I fed was all huddled together," Gus said. "Keeping each other warm."

"Yeah, they were. The snow is really coming down again, but this line doesn't look as bad as the last one, so hopefully we're coming to the end of this. It would sure be nice if it would stop, so we could get a break." Haven reached for the bread, took what he wanted, and passed it on. "Make sure there's wood in the bunkhouse. You all know how the power can go out when it gets windy like this."

"I already did," Gus said with a smile. "And there's more right outside the door, just in case." He went back to eating, and the general conversation died away. Brian shifted in his seat and glanced at the other men. He found himself wondering about each of them. Were they gay too? It didn't matter, but he couldn't help being curious. Then his attention settled on David. He ate slowly and kept glancing at David, but sometimes he was seeing the high school kid from his memory.

In his mind's eye, Brian could see David strolling down the old white halls lined with green lockers in the senior section of the building. He had perpetually seemed like a senior to Brian. David had always been on the top of the high school world. Cheerleaders laughed at his jokes and walked with him down the halls. There was always a smile on his face and a swagger in his step.

But that smile was gone now, replaced with small lines around his mouth and eyes, and from what Brian saw, the internal light that everyone had been attracted to back then, that indeterminate thing that made Brian and everyone else want to get close to David, seemed to have gone out. He was like everyone else. Well, sort of. The other guys talked and laughed, nudging each other and sharing jokes. David seemed to be on the outside of all that. No one leaned over to share a funny story with him or stopped to nudge his shoulder when someone else said something funny. David simply sat there and ate, staying out of the conversation. Quiet. Almost as quiet as Brian.

The soup was good, and after a while, Brian pulled his attention away from David and settled it back on his lunch. He had some salad and bread, filling his belly, the hunger that had seemed ever-present for the past week abating for a while.

Brian was tired. The excitement of the morning and the fact that he hadn't slept well for days worrying about his next meal and his next bed was all catching up to him. For right now, at least, he had a warm place to stay and regular meals. The guys would probably help him get his car out of the ditch and he'd need to get gas somehow, but after that and Dakota checking out his feet, he'd be on his way again.

Laughter broke out, with everyone joining in, even David. Brian had completely missed the joke and wondered for a second if he was the butt of the joke. But no one looked at him, except maybe David, who only glanced away again whenever Brian glanced at him. That little movement put a smile on his face: David remembered him. Back when they'd been kids, Brian had been a nobody, the kid of one of the ranch hands. The people at the top of the ladder were the wealthier kids from town and then the kids of ranch owners, not the sons of the foremen.

Brian had been a pretty good student. His dad had expected him to do well, and Brian had. At one point, he had thought about trying to go to college, but there was no money for it, and after his rodeo dreams failed, Brian simply fell into ranch life. It was what he knew.

The men began getting up from the table, pulling Brian out of his memories. They all thanked Phillip and pulled on their cold weather gear before heading back outside. There was always work to do, even on days like this. Barns could be cleaned, and there was tack to be mended and equipment to work on, as long as it was inside. And, of course, weather like this brought its own set of challenges. Packed and drifted snow formed ramps over fences, freezing and thawing fence posts, bringing them down. On a ranch, there was no end to the work, winter or summer. That was one of the few things that could be counted on.

"Would you like some more?" Phillip asked.

Brian was stuffed and as content as he'd been in a while. "No, thank you. It was very good." He finished the last little bit in his bowl and then stood and carried his dishes over. Phillip scolded him lightly, and he sat back down.

"So you knew David?" Phillip asked as he worked.

"Yeah, back in school. No big deal," Brian said.

Phillip paused, holding a dish above the sink. "Okay," he said and then went back to his work. "Were you friends?"

"No," Brian answered and shook his head. "He was the star athlete. I was just a kid." He got up and brought the salad bowl and hardly touched veggie plate to the counter. "Not a big hit, was it?" Brian said, looking at where the carrots had been picked at but nothing else touched.

"Well… all they want to eat is meat, and that isn't good, so I always put one out. They each take a little to be polite and that's about it. But the way I look at it, I got a few raw vegetables in them." He covered the plate and put it away. "It's a losing battle, but what the heck. Someday they'll thank me, when they don't get cancer or something." Phillip smiled and continued putting things away. Then he loaded the dishwasher and got it going. "I've got some work to do. You're welcome to watch television or lie down if you want. You look dead on your feet." Phillip motioned toward the hall, and Brian followed him.

The guest room was clean and bright, with light gray walls, white furniture, and pictures of a horse, a lion, and a herd of cattle on the walls. "Is that one of Wally's?"

"Yeah," Phillip said and pointed to another. Brian hadn't believed it, but there was visual proof: a lion getting his belly scratched. "I'll let you get comfortable. If you need me, I'll be in the office, off the hall back toward the living room. The bathroom is right across the hall. There are towels and things if you want to shower. I suggest doing it right away. I don't know how much longer the power is going to last."

A beep sounded from the kitchen. Phillip headed that way, leaving him alone. A pair of sweatpants and a T-shirt had been placed on the bed, so Brian picked them up and went to the bathroom. It was warm, and he closed the door. He caught his reflection in the mirror. He looked like hell. There were bags under his eyes and his skin was all red, probably from the cold. He hadn't shaved regularly, so he was scruffy and shaggy as shit. He went back to the bedroom and found his backpack by the bed. He grabbed it and returned to the bathroom, where he shaved, and then showered quickly. It felt good to be clean, and he looked a lot less like something the cat dragged in.

The clean clothes were nice and smelled fresh. He didn't have fresh socks, but he found a pair on the bed when he returned to the room. Brian figured he'd stay out of the way, so he climbed into bed and pulled the spread over himself. He was asleep almost before he realized he'd closed his eyes.

Chapter Two

DAVID WAS working in the barn. He checked on all the horses and other animals, listening to the wind as it whistled outside. The animals seemed content, which to David was always a good sign. If they were restless and jittery, then something was coming. They were calm and munching happily at their hay. Even on a cold, snowy, windy day like today, the barn was relatively warm and cozy with the heat from the animals.

He went to the tack room and made sure everything was in its proper place. There was mending to be done, so he set all that aside. One of his jobs was fixing tack. At least on days like this it gave him something to do inside. Equipment rumbled past outside as snow was cleared and the driveway plowed. They would most likely have to do that multiple times.

"Where do you want the blow-in's car?" Gus asked with a grin as he came into the room. "I can't find Haven, and I got it pulled out of the snowbank."

"Is there a clear space up near the house? If there is, put it there," David answered with a smile. For some reason the guys came to him with questions. David had no idea why, but they did. Most of the men didn't talk to him much, like they did among themselves, but they asked him questions all the time.

"So, you know that guy you rescued? Was he one of your boot knockers?" Gus asked, and David shook his head.

"Brian and I went to high school together. There was nothing like that between us. Why, do you like him?"

Gus's mouth dropped open in shock. The man was a huge softie and had a girlfriend he thought the world of. He also wasn't the brightest bulb on the string, but he was loyal, worked hard, and really cared about the people he worked with. Gus was a gentle giant if David had ever met one.

"I'm just teasing," David said. "He's someone I remember from my hometown." David sighed and went back to work. Gus stuck around for a few minutes and then left the barn. David remembered Brian as the quiet kid in math class with long, black poodle hair falling in his face all the time. David had been the captain of the football team, and he'd always been surrounded by people. Brian had been just the opposite, and maybe that had been what caught David's attention. That and the fact that Brian was really cute. Not so much in a way that girls noticed—he wasn't handsome or charming—but he'd had a look about him that appealed to David. That had been a long time ago, in a different time—hell, a different life. And it didn't matter how cute Brian had been or if those same qualities that David remembered were still there. David had spent way too much time and energy on men. He'd spent enough that he'd screwed up his life and messed up the one good thing he'd ever been able to find.

Mario had loved him, and David had thrown that away to follow his dick to greener pastures. He'd gotten restless, and instead of sticking things out and making them work, he'd left with some kid, who in turn had left him. That one stupid decision had cost him Mario, and his home, and he'd ended up coming back here with his tail between his legs. To make matters worse, once he'd realized what he truly wanted, it was too late. Mario had found Gordon, and the two of them were happy as anything. Part of him was happy for Mario, but it had taken him a long time to reach that place. Most of the people on the ranch still resented him for leaving in the first place. Wally certainly did. He hadn't spoken to him other than a few times to be polite since he'd got back, and he had made it clear that David was to stay here and work on this portion of the ranch. David had hoped that, with Mario happy, Wally would get over it and his attitude would thaw. But that hadn't happened yet, and David was starting to wonder if it ever would.

"How much more do you have to do?" Haven asked from the doorway, startling David slightly. "The weather is getting worse, so make sure everything is buttoned up in here and that all the animals have everything they need. Then we can call it a day." They had been going since dawn, trying to get things done before the storm and then during the break in the snow. Pulling a stray out of a snowbank had taken precious time from the day. "I just hope this weather pattern shifts soon. If we get much more of this, the snow will be so deep the cattle won't be able to move and we'll start to lose them. They can take a lot, but I'm afraid the herd is starting to reach that limit."

"It's supposed to warm up in a few days. They said even above freezing, so some of this could melt," David offered.

"It will, and what remains will get wetter and heavier before refreezing again. This has been a tough winter, and I'm afraid it will get tougher before it gets easier." Haven turned back toward the door. "When you're done, come up to the house if you want."

"How's the guy we rescued?" David asked.

"Last I heard from Phillip, he's sleeping." Haven turned and walked back. "It seems we found him just in time. Apparently he was on the verge of frostbite, and as cold and windy as it was, he wouldn't have lasted much longer. Did you really know him once?"

"Yup. We went to high school together," David said. "Did Phillip get out of him why he was out here on a day like this?"

"You'll have to ask him," Haven answered and hurried toward the barn door. David wondered if Haven meant asking Phillip or Brian, but he was gone before he could clarify. He sighed and did another check on the horses, adding hay to mangers and then filling water troughs with warm water. It was warm enough that the water wouldn't freeze, but it would be easier on the horses if they weren't drinking such cold water. Warm water helped them maintain internal temperature. Once he was done, David fed the dogs and ensured they had a warm place to sleep. Then he pulled open the barn door and went out, closing it again against the wind, which whipped around him. It seemed to try to find any place it could to reach his skin.

Snow continued to come down, and David rushed across the yard to the door of the house. He opened it and went right inside. On days like this, no one stood on ceremony. He took off his boots and hung up his coat in the small laundry room.

"Come on in and sit down," Phillip said from the living area. There was a fire already burning in the stove, and Phillip opened it to put in another piece of wood. "Didn't know how much longer we'd have power and heat, so I figured I'd make sure we were ready." The ranch had generators, but they were limited and only to be used for essentials. Anything that took a load off them meant the fuel lasted longer.

"Do you need me to bring in any more wood?" David asked.

"No. There's plenty for the rest of the day and tonight. Sit down and relax," Phillip offered, and David took a seat on the sofa. He couldn't help glancing around, and then he saw Phillip watching him.

"Was there something you needed?" After work, he'd just expected to go back to the bunkhouse with the other guys. He wondered how Brian was doing, but couldn't think of a good way to ask.

"No," Phillip said. "Brian is sleeping."

David nodded at the answer to his unasked question. "Is he going to be all right?" He tried to sound concerned but not too concerned.

"I believe so, yes," Phillip answered and then stood up. "I'll be right back. Just relax." Phillip handed him the remote control off the table. "You can watch something if you like. We might as well get comfortable. With this weather, we aren't likely to be going anywhere anytime soon." He left the room, and David absently turned on the television. He found a station showing an old black-and-white movie and settled in to watch. Phillip returned with a tray and set it on the table. "I figured hot coffee would be in order on a day like this."

Haven came in, closing the door behind him with a thud. "Dang, it's still snowing, but I think the wind is finally starting to die down."

Phillip got up and hurried over to where Haven was pulling off his coat and hat. They shared a kiss, and as soon as Haven had his coat off, they shared a genuinely warm hug. "You're cold," Phillip whispered, and David turned away. It seemed like an invasion of privacy to watch them. They were so happy together. The old want surfaced. He wanted what they had, but then the realization bloomed once again that he'd had that and thrown it away. David knew he didn't deserve to be happy again, not like that. He'd screwed up and caused himself and Mario a great deal of pain. Three years they were together, and he couldn't be satisfied. Mario had loved him, and he had loved Mario. They could have had a good life, but instead of seeing things through or working at it when they began to grow apart, he had let his eye wander and fallen for someone else.

"Fuck," David said under his breath. He knew that was only part of the story. He and Mario *had* grown apart; they had both known that.

"Brian," Phillip said, and David turned to see the other man standing at the entrance to the room. He was wearing what looked like a purple T-shirt that could only have come from Phillip. No one else on the ranch would ever wear anything like that. Brian also had on a pair of gray sweatpants that hugged his slim hips. He looked just like David remembered from high school. Brian's eyes still had that hint of mischief and the blue was richer than in his mind's eye. There were lines that hadn't been on Brian's teenage face, but it was most definitely him. David tried to figure out why he hadn't recognized him right away and realized it was the hair. Brian's hair was shorter now. It had probably been a while since he'd had it cut, but the curls were gone.

"Sorry I was out so long," Brian said as he came into the room and looked around.

"I washed your clothes for you. I'll put the basket and the rest of your things in your room," Phillip said and hustled out of the room. David shook his head. In all the time he'd known Phillip, he seemed to do everything like he was hyped on caffeine. The only time he didn't was when he was working on the books. Then he was quiet and could sit for hours, but otherwise he always ran at full speed.

Haven motioned for Brian to have a seat, and Brian sat on the other end of the sofa from David. "You came really close to hypothermia," Haven said. "I'm glad we found you in time."

"I am too," Brian said, but there was no conviction in his voice. It was like he said the words because he thought he was supposed to rather than because he meant them.

David turned to look at him and paused. He'd seen that same expression before, in the mirror about six months ago, when he'd come back: complete lack of hope. Brian had given up and hadn't really cared if he'd been found. He'd curled up on the backseat to die. The thought sent a cold chill through David from head to toe. He knew exactly how it felt to be at the end of his rope and what he'd had to do with the help of friends to try to build a life again.

"I wasn't sure where I was going and got all turned around," Brian said. "I was just hoping someone lived down this way because of the sign at the corner." He stared down at his sock feet.

"Well, we're glad we found you in time," Haven said. He got up and left the room, calling out to Phillip that he'd meet him in the kitchen.

"Are you really all right?"

"Yeah, I'm okay." Brian swallowed. "I can't believe it was you who helped me. I haven't seen you in, what, almost fourteen years or something."

"Yeah." David said. He hadn't thought about Brian in years, but the memories were still pretty vivid. "It's been a long time, and we're both a ways from home."

"Yeah, well, I don't have a home to go back to, and now I don't have a job and I'm as broke as anyone can get." Brian shifted. "I had a good place, but... who I was got in the way, and they decided I wasn't worth the effort."

David had experienced the same sort of thing over the years. The people he came across tended to be conservative, and ranches were notoriously testosterone-driven places. Guys spent a lot of time together, living and working in close quarters for long periods. They wanted to know that the guys they were working with weren't watching them. The best place he'd ever worked was here on the ranch, and he'd given it up. The only good thing to happen to him had been their allowing him to come back. It hadn't been easy, and his ex had actually stepped in and stood up for him, which was more than he'd had a right to expect. But Mario was a good man, David knew that, and he was forever out of David's grasp. "I've been there. I think most of the guys on the ranch, at least the gay ones, have been through that."

"So everyone isn't gay?" Brian asked.

"No. Lots of the guys aren't. But Haven and Dakota don't stand for any trouble. They hire the best people and treat them well. Like family." That was why it had hurt so much when he'd left and then come back. Not only had he left the ranch, but he had left his family behind. That was what he hadn't understood until he was gone, and that was why he'd come back. "They're the best here."

Brian nodded but didn't look up from his feet. "I asked Phillip for a job, but it's winter and I know most places don't have positions, not this time of year." Brian sighed. "He did say to talk to Haven and Dakota, and I will when he comes over to look at me tomorrow, but I'm not really holding out much hope." He finally lifted his gaze. "But this place seems like heaven."

"Just be honest with them. Dakota is a good guy, and so is Haven. They took me in after I... when I needed a place desperately. They have a history of helping people. Heck, half the guys who work at Dakota's are people they've helped. And if there isn't a place here, they know everybody in the area. They'll be able to help."

Brian didn't say anything and didn't react much. He simply looked up blankly and then went back to staring at his feet. David watched and waited. It had been more than a decade since he'd seen Brian, but something in him stirred David's compassion. Maybe it was the fact that he'd been where Brian was now not long ago. His mother, bless her departed soul, would probably have said something about first love and how powerful it was. David wasn't sure he bought that. Hell, he'd noticed Brian in school and he'd watched him sometimes, but he doubted Brian had been his first love. They really hadn't talked much other than....

"I don't know if anyone can help," Brian finally said. "But I'm going to ask. It can't hurt. I have skills and I'm a hard worker. No one ever accused me of shirking anything." Brian met his gaze, and determination blazed for a second before fading away. Whatever had happened to Brian had touched him deeply. But it didn't appear he was ready to talk about it. And David wasn't going to press. He'd learned a long time ago that guys deserved their privacy and that most people had their secrets. David had his, just like anyone else, and he didn't want them broadcast for everyone to know. Not that his were all that serious, just stuff he wasn't particularly proud of.

There was a tradition out in the West. See, it was modern, and they had all the conveniences, but on the range, away from cities, where it was wide-open land, Mother Nature still ruled, the heartless bitch, and it could still be a battle every day for survival. That bred tough people, and those people held their cards close to the vest. It was part of the cowboy DNA. "What sort of skills do you have?" he asked Brian.

"I'm good with horses and cattle, animals in general, I guess. I've been doing ranch work since I was a kid. I used to make tack and stuff, so I'm really good with the leather. I told Phillip I don't have any tools anymore, but I could get some."

"Hallelujah," David said. "That's one of the things I do, and I'm passable at it, but not an expert or anything. Folks always need that work done. Maybe if you work here, they could set you up with a shop or something."

"Why?"

David scooted to the edge of the sofa. "People here have got all kinds of skills. Dakota's a doctor, but you know that. His partner Wally's a vet. He has an office on the other part of the ranch. Dakota built it for him. It's where he and Liam, his assistant, keep all the animal records and where Wally sees patients when people bring in dogs and cats, smaller animals. The big animals Wally goes to."

"It sounds ideal," Brian said.

David took a deep breath. "It is. Dakota and his dad started the ranch, and Haven added his land years ago. Jefferson, Dakota's dad, was an amazing man. Everyone loved him. And it's his way of doing things that we all stick to. People are treated with respect, and they're encouraged. It's like we're all one big family." David paused. "I think you'll find that a lot of the guys here, straight or gay, have had a tough time at one point or another."

Brian nodded gently, and Phillip came back in the room with Haven. They sat down and settled their gazes on Brian.

"How are you feeling now?" Haven asked. "No residual numbness in your feet and hands?"

"No. I'm really good." Brian lifted his gaze. "I want to thank you for finding me and for getting my car out of the ditch. I don't have much to repay you with...." He looked back down again. Hell, it had to be obvious to everyone in the room that Brian didn't have two sticks to rub together.

"Look," Haven began. "We don't really need another hand. We're full up right now."

"I understand. It's a bad time of year to be looking for work."

"That it is, and we know that. So we ain't going to put you out in the cold. We just can't do that. We won't. There's room in the bunkhouse, and tomorrow you can move in there. I don't know what I'm going to have you do at first, other than help where needed, but we'll see to it that you're fed and have a warm place. Who knows, when this weather breaks—God willing, it's soon—there will be plenty of work."

"Thank you," he whispered.

The scent of roasting meat decided to make an appearance, and David's stomach growled loudly. Dang, that smelled good.

"I put a ham in the oven. It should be done in half an hour or so," Phillip explained. "Before I came here, I could burn water."

Haven chuckled and tugged Phillip to him. "Before you came here, you wore jeans with sparkles on the butt."

Phillip laughed. "I still have those jeans. Maybe I'll wear them for you if you're good."

Brian excused himself and left the room, heading toward the bathroom. Phillip watched him go, then glanced at Haven and then at David. "Thanks for helping him," Phillip said to Haven.

"He seems to have had a round of bad luck," David said.

"He told me a little about it," Phillip said and turned to look where Brian had gone. "I get the feeling there's more to it than he's saying."

"There's always more to it. He's a cowboy, and this is a hard life. You don't do it because you're full of sunshine and flowers. It takes a tough person, and that toughness comes with cuts, scrapes, and a lot of scars. He has them, the same as the rest of us. For now, as long as he don't cause trouble and is willing to help out, we'll have a place for him. But we still gotta keep an eye on him." Haven quieted, and seconds later a door opened and closed, then Brian came back in the room and sat down.

"So what have you been doing since high school?" David asked. He needed something to start the conversation, and it was all he could think of.

Brian shrugged. "I left home right after graduation. I was going to be a rodeo star. Ride bulls and be famous. That was my plan."

"Aren't you a little tall for that?" David asked.

"Yeah. That was part of the disappointment. I graduated and joined the rodeo circuit, but the problem was that I continued to grow. I got too tall to ride bulls, so I switched to broncos. I was pretty good, but I was never going to be great. It seemed my quest to be famous turned out like a lot of the other things I tried to do. In the end I got hired on at a ranch and started doing what I'd done all my life."

"As I remember, you were really smart. Did you think about college?"

"I did. But we couldn't afford it. Three brothers, two sisters, and nothing really saved up. I knew it didn't matter how smart I was, I had to go out and get a job once I was old enough. It was expected. So that's what I did."

"Did your folks kick you out when they found out you were gay?" David asked.

Brian shook his head. "They were real disappointed, but they didn't disown me or anything. The relationship wasn't the same, though. We didn't know how to talk to each other, and by then I'd been on my own for a few years, so it didn't seem to matter as much. I had a job and was making my own way, so they let me be, most of the time." Brian paused. "What about you?"

"Pretty much the same, I guess. My mom and dad never understood me being gay, so we don't talk much, usually just holidays and birthdays. Sometimes I think things are getting better, but...." He shrugged. "I worked in Montana for a while, but this is home." David really didn't want to talk about himself.

It was still painful and only acted as a reminder of how foolish he'd been.

David hoped Phillip and Haven would add to the conversation, but they were whispering back and forth, off in their own little love-nest world. Eventually they left the room, and David tried to think of something for him and Brian to talk about.

The room got quiet and the whistle of the wind provided most of the sound. "I used to hate that wind," Brian said eventually. "I watched the *Wizard of Oz* when I was a kid. I was always afraid that the wind was going to pick the house up and carry us all away." There was a hint of mischief in Brian's voice. "Then, as I got older, I used to tease my younger sisters about it. They'd squeal and run to Mama." Brian smiled slightly as his expression warmed. "I haven't seen any of them in a long time."

"Don't you talk to any of them?" David asked.

"Not really, not anymore. Things fell apart after my dad died some time ago. Mom never really understood the whole gay thing, like your folks, and she had the girls to take care of, so she ended up moving to Maryland to be near her family. I wasn't invited to go, so I haven't seen any of them since then. I couldn't afford to take the time off or pay to travel to visit, and well, while they never said anything, I wasn't sure I'd really be welcome." Brian sighed softly. "I made my decisions and was living my own life, so I just went on doing it."

"Sounds lonely," David observed from personal experience.

"Yeah, it pretty much was... and is. I had a guy I thought was a boyfriend and I really liked him, but it turned out he was interested in... what I could do for him, if you know what I mean."

David did, and he nodded. "Is that why you had to leave the other place? I mean, did that contribute to you getting fired?"

"No. That was a while ago."

The scent of dinner got stronger and stronger, making David's mouth water, but he focused his attention on Brian and off his belly as best he could.

"The stuff that got me fired was different... and the same, I guess." Brian stood up. "Why do guys have to be such jackasses?" He whirled around. "They act all nice when they want something, and then turn on you as soon as they... well, you get the picture. They think with their dicks and nothing else."

David winced at that. It was true; he couldn't deny it. He'd done exactly that.

"I've decided that no matter where I land, I'm not going to let sex get in the way anymore. I don't need to get involved, and I certainly don't need to be on the lookout for love." Brian rolled his eyes. "That only leads to trouble, no matter what happened with the two lovebirds in there."

David laughed. "They caused plenty of trouble in their day, if I'm not mistaken," David said. "And I don't blame you for feeling that way."

"Guys, come to the table," Phillip called, cutting off David's thought. They headed into the kitchen and sat down. The wind whipped around the house and the lights flickered, then went dark.

"I got the lamps ready in the laundry room," Phillip said, and soon Haven had an oil lamp lit and placed on the table. David went back into the living room and put another log on the fire. It was going to get pretty cold in the house.

"Do you need help getting the generators running?" David asked Haven as the phone began to ring. Haven nodded, and David went to get his gear.

"You can take fifteen minutes to eat while the food is hot," Phillip scolded both of them. "They aren't going anywhere."

"Okay," Haven said and sat down, talking briefly to Dakota before hanging up. "Dakota has called in the outage, but it will most likely be sometime tomorrow before we get power again. There isn't that much that we need to run, but it would be nice to have some heat."

"We'll be fine," Phillip said and brought the last of the food to the table. "Now go ahead and eat. If you're going back out in the cold, you might as well have a full stomach." Sometimes Phillip sounded like a mother hen, just like Wally could when he wanted to.

"I know," Haven said indulgently and began filling his plate. "What are you doing?" Haven asked when Phillip pulled out his phone.

"Calling over to the bunkhouse to make sure the men are okay." Phillip talked briefly to whoever answered and then hung up. "They're fine and said they were cooking there rather than brave the cold again."

"Good," Haven said and tilted his head toward the chair. Phillip sat down, and they all began to eat. It was surprisingly nice to eat by lamplight. David had often wondered what the lives of original settlers of this area had been like. They would have had lamps for light and fires for heat, just like they were using now. Of course, the house would have been much smaller, with less space to heat.

"This is good, thank you," Brian said to Phillip. "I really appreciate the hospitality."

"You're very welcome," Phillip said.

"But don't get used to it," Haven said with a smile. "Phillip hates to cook. He's allowed me to press him into service because of the weather and the fact that I told him if he cooked, he wouldn't have to help outdoors. But this is not how we usually eat."

"Then who cooks?" Brian asked.

"Haven, usually," Phillip explained. "He's a very good cook. Mostly today I've been following his instructions."

David saw Brian look at both of them as though he was trying to puzzle something out.

"I don't understand. I thought you were the—" Brian stopped.

Phillip leaned over the table slightly. "If you were about to say you thought I was the lady of the house, you can get rid of that notion. Haven and I are partners. We do things equally, and we share. Long ago we figured out he's a much better cook than I am, but I do the laundry and stuff like that, because if I didn't, Haven would bleach every shred of clothing both of us owned stark white." Phillip bumped Haven's shoulder. "It isn't the same for everyone, but it works for the two of us."

"Okay," Brian said.

"Like I said, it's a partnership. There are things we each do well and things each of us hates to do. We worked it out a long time ago, and it's good for us." Phillip sat back. "In relationships like ours there isn't someone who acts like the man and another who acts like the woman—it doesn't work that way, or it doesn't have to work that way. It works however the two people are comfortable."

Brian nodded and went back to eating. He didn't say much after that, and David wondered if Phillip had hurt his feelings. Phillip's phone rang and he talked with someone briefly.

"Just a minute," Phillip said and turned to Haven. "Gus has the bunkhouse generator going and everything is fine there. He's asking if you want him to get the house one up and running as well."

"Tell him I'll take care of it. The one here is touchier because of its size. He should go back inside where it's warm, but if he wants to do us a favor, ask him to check the barn. I just want to make sure it isn't too cold in there."

"I put blankets on the horses before I left. I figured with this wind it was best to be safe," David explained, and Haven nodded and smiled. Phillip relayed the message and hung up. They spent the next ten minutes finishing dinner. Brian said very little, which concerned David. He remembered Brian as quiet, but this was too quiet. He seemed introspective. When Haven set down the saltshaker a little sharply on the table, Brian jumped. What could have made him so nervous all the time? Maybe he'd been through something traumatic, something other than what had just happened.

David began clearing the plates once the meal was over.

"I can help with the dishes," Brian said.

"Will you give me a hand?" Haven asked David, and David stopped what he was doing, thanked Brian for his offer, and began getting on his gear to go outside.

"I'll turn off the lights and things as soon as the power comes on. I've already made sure the stove is off so it won't pull all the power."

"Thanks, hon," Haven said gently and leaned close to give Phillip a light kiss. Haven whispered something to Phillip, and David saw him color. "Build up the fire. We're going to need it tonight. David and I will go get the generator started." Phillip nodded quickly.

"Let's get this cleaned up so we can go sit where it's warm," Phillip said to Brian as David finished getting into his gear.

Ten minutes later he and Haven braved the cold to the small shed in back. David made sure the generator tank was full, and Haven began the process of starting it. The batteries for the electric starter were cold and would be low on power because of it. "I've got everything ready. Let's give it a try. We only get one shot and then we'll have to pull." Haven pressed the button, and thankfully the engine cranked, turned over, and then caught, roaring to life, filling the small shed with noise. David peered out the door and looked toward the house, where light blazed in the windows. Then one by one, some of the windows went dark.

"Is there power?" Haven asked.

"Yes," David answered.

"Good. I have the switch set so as soon as the power comes back on, the generator will stop." Haven closed the lid on the generator casing. "Let's get back to the house. My hands ache already." Haven left the shed and closed the door. They strode through the snow back along the path they'd created on their way to the shed. When they got in the house, the first thing David noticed was the heat that blew at him. It was glorious. He took off his things and wondered if he should simply go back to the bunkhouse.

"I have coffee in here," Phillip said. "It's decaf, but it'll warm you."

David hung up his coat and joined the others in the living room. The stove fire blazed and the room was warm and inviting. He sat next to Brian as Haven and Phillip settled together on the rug on the floor. They were so natural together, it made David long for something he knew he shouldn't want. He'd already had it once and knew that was his one opportunity, his only one. He didn't have a right to expect or even dream of another.

"What do you do here besides take care of the tack?" Brian asked.

"I'm a general cowboy, I guess. I mainly take care of the horses, though. The barn is largely my domain, although I do work with the herds and do other things when it's needed. Like most places, we do what needs to be done. We're big enough that most people have daily duties they're responsible for, but not big enough that that's all anyone does. If there's a fence down and cattle are loose, then everyone pitches in to help."

Brian nodded. "It seems like a good place."

Haven looked up at both of them. "We try to make it the best place to work in this area of the state. Dakota once said that folks won't care if you're different as long as you treat them with respect, pay a good wage, and make sure everyone is treated the same. So far he's been right, and I don't see that changing anytime soon." Haven smiled at Brian and turned back to the fire.

"That's pretty much what I did at my last place," Brian said. "How many head do you have here?"

"All told, about fifteen hundred head. The herd has been growing the past few years, and that's been very good for all of us," Haven explained. "The ranch has its own natural water supply, so even in the worst drought, like we had a few years ago, we were able to keep growing."

"You're very lucky. My last place didn't have that. They relied on wells that got dangerously low and they had to sell some of the stock early so we didn't run out of water."

Haven nodded slowly. "A lot of the spreads had to do that. The water access is largely due to Jefferson and my father being long-sighted. They bought land no one else wanted years ago, when it wasn't so much of an issue. That purchase guaranteed them water rights that we use to this day." Haven shifted. "We are very careful, though. We pump the water to the cattle and keep them a good distance away to help protect the stream from runoff. We've even constructed low berms to help ensure cattle waste doesn't wash directly into the stream. It helps with the long-term viability of the water supply. We've also helped the ranches upstream do the same."

"Do you have troubles with wolves?" Brian asked. "We did at my last place."

"We used to. But Wally's cats tend to keep them away. The lions, in particular, do not like wolves at all. When they cry to each other, Wally says that the lions answer with roars that split the night sometimes. Then all is quiet. We had a few bold enough a few years ago to get curious. One got too close to the lions' and tigers' cages and we found what was left of it after one of the tigers got its claws into it. Shahrazad was one mean bitch. Wally doesn't have her any longer. She's in a zoo, probably terrorizing all the other animals."

"Cattle, horses, lions, and tigers—what else do you guys have?"

"Some dogs," David said. "Wally has a few other animals he's rescued from circuses and other places. It's in his nature. He'll help any animal that needs him."

"He even nursed a wolf back to health and then released her. Dakota was ready to spit nails at the time. They apparently fought over it, but Wally stood his ground and threatened to leave. He and Dakota still don't see eye to eye on the wolf issue, but Wally agreed not to rescue any more and Dakota doesn't allow the men to shoot them on sight. Not that we've seen any lately.

"Although given how tough this winter is getting, I suspect we will before long. They'll get desperate and begin to encroach," Haven said and turned back to Phillip. "I need to remember to talk to all the men about it. We need to keep a lookout for any signs of them. With this much snow, the herd will be sitting ducks, since they won't be able to move very well."

The conversation quieted and everyone drank their coffee and watched the flames. David kept glancing at Brian, watching the flames dance in his eyes. Suddenly he was transported down memory lane, back to high school. He remembered how sure of himself he'd been. At the time, he'd had everything. He was popular and thought he knew all the answers to whatever the world would throw at him. He was sitting on top of the world and knew it. Or at least he thought he'd been. He hadn't bothered to really get to know people he thought were beneath him. After all, he was the captain of the football team, the star player. The guy everyone wanted to know or be like.

That had been a long time ago, and he was nothing like that now. Oh, he wanted to be. That was why he'd followed his cock to some excited kid. Colton had been young and he'd hung on everything David had said. And David had let himself think that was the way he should be treated rather than being in a committed relationship as equals. His ego and hubris had caused him to end the best relationship he'd ever had.

He could see Brian the way he'd been back in school. David had noticed him because he was cute. But he'd never approached him or included him in his circle of friends. Now he wished he had. Brian turned his head slightly and saw David staring at him. David didn't look away. He wanted Brian to know that he'd been looking, watching him.

Brian tilted his head slightly in a silent question, and David smiled. He saw the amusement in Brian's eyes, and it made his stomach do a little flip. Brian's smile broadened and he turned back toward David once again. David smiled in response. He couldn't help it. Brian made him want to. Hell, he wanted to laugh and shout as he bathed in the glow of Brian's simple but sincere smile.

Phillip stood up and Haven did the same. "We all need to get to bed. There will be plenty to do tomorrow, and we're going to need to be up early."

Haven nodded. "We're going to have one hell of a day digging out of this storm."

David said good night and got his gear. He put it on and left the house, then hurried across the yard to the bunkhouse. Inside, most of the men were still up, but they seemed to be making the move to bed. David said his good-nights, went to his small room, and closed the door. There was heat from the generator, and he grabbed his kit and hurried to the bathroom to get ready before the rush. He cleaned up and then went back to his room. A few others were milling about. Some had headed to their rooms, and others were still sitting out by the woodstove. The house wasn't particularly warm, but it wasn't cold either. On a night like this, they needed to keep the fire going. Gus placed wood in the stove and then closed the door and adjusted the air intake so the wood would burn more slowly into the night.

David told him good night and closed his door. He undressed and got into bed. He wanted to simply fall asleep, but of course he couldn't. His mind kept going back to Brian and then over all the things he'd wished he'd done differently. He thought about what a self-centered asshole he'd been when he was a kid. He'd always thought he'd outgrown that, but he was wrong. It was that attitude that had led him to leave Mario. He'd like to think he was different now, but he wasn't so sure.

David tossed and turned in his bed while he listened as the others moved through the bunkhouse. Slowly it got quieter, and eventually the light coming in under his door went out. The generator kicked the heat on every once in a while, filling the room with warmth. But the temperature fluctuated wildly, and David went from being cold to warm and back again. Eventually, he got up, wrapped the spread around his shoulders, and headed for the living area. He sat in one of the big chairs and pulled his feet under the spread. It was warm and surprisingly comfortable. He stared at the stove and then got up and slowly opened the door so he could watch the flames.

"Is something wrong?" Gus asked from behind him. David hadn't heard him come in.

"No. I just couldn't sleep," he answered without looking away from the flames. They seemed to settle his thoughts and stop his mind from running in circles.

Gus walked away and returned a few minutes later with a homemade patchwork quilt—yellow, with little sunflower boys on it—wrapped around his shoulders. David smiled. "My grandmother made it for me when I was six years old," Gus said. "It's the only thing I have left of her, so I keep it on my bed." He smiled. "It was made with love and that's how I always feel when I use it."

"I'm the last one to disparage anyone for a quilt or anything else," David said. "It would be nice if I had something my grandmother made for me." David turned his gaze back to the fire.

"Why are you thinking so hard?" Gus asked.

"I don't know. I think meeting Brian made me think about all the things I did in high school, and afterward. I wasn't a very nice person."

"Oh," Gus said. David settled a little lower in his seat and stretched out his legs, the fire keeping his feet warm. "Everybody was kinda dumb in high school. We all thought we had things figured out. But none of us really did. The brains thought they owned the world, but some of them didn't go anywhere. The jocks figured they ruled the school, but after we graduated, they faded to nothing and will probably spend the rest of their lives reliving their glory days."

"Yeah. That's it exactly. Except some of us continue to think things haven't changed," David said with a sigh.

"We all want to be Peter Pan," Gus said. "My grandmother used to read me that story when I was little. I always wanted to be able to fly and go wherever I wanted. We all have to grow up, and none of us can change the past. We only get to affect our future."

"You're very wise," David said, fully aware that Gus was just the kind of guy he would have ignored in school unless he'd been a member of the football team.

"I'm prob'ly the dumbest guy here," Gus said. He tended to be a little slow on the uptake sometimes, but he had a heart to match the rest of him. "I never finished school and...."

"Hey. You know horses and cattle better than almost anyone, and the things that need to be done here on the ranch? You know it all. That's what counts."

"Yeah, well...." Gus pulled the quilt a little tighter around his broad shoulders. "When I first came here, I didn't like working for people like Haven and Dakota. My mama always told me people like them were bad. Grandma too."

"It was the way they were raised, and the way they raised you."

"Yeah. That's just it. They taught me how to act and stuff. But it took me a while to learn that they weren't always right, just like you aren't always right." Gus nodded. "Nobody is right all the time." Gus shifted his gaze away from the flames. "Especially when we're kids. We get stuff wrong all the time. I did."

"Yeah," David whispered. "Like I said, you're a wise man."

"I don't get what you mean," Gus said. "I ain't smart and you know it." There was an edge to his voice, and David realized Gus must have thought David was picking on him.

"Smart people know the answers to questions. But it's wise people who help others find their answers. And you're a wise man. Don't ever let anyone tell you otherwise." David stood up. "I think I'm going to head off to bed now. You should probably do the same. It's getting late, and there will be a lot to do tomorrow. It's supposed to be cold and sunny, which means we're going to have to figure out how to dig our way through all this mess." Gus stood as well, and David smiled. He placed another log in the stove and adjusted the air intake while Gus headed back to his room. He felt much better about a lot of things. David turned and watched as Gus disappeared into his room, looking at the huge and usually relatively quiet man with different eyes. He needed to do more of that—accept and look at people for who they were and what their strengths were, rather than how they fit into his obviously skewed worldview.

David sighed softly and shook his head. All of this seemed like a bit much for a cowboy like him. He'd been thinking way too much about crap he couldn't do shit about. Gus was right— the past was the past, but if he wanted things to be different, then he needed to worry about changing the future. His future. He just wished he knew how in hell to go about it.

Chapter Three

BRIAN SPENT much of the night thinking about the fact that, for now, he had a job of sorts. They were going to give him a place to stay and what seemed like a chance to prove himself. It was pretty plain that there wasn't going to be a repeat of the troubles he'd had at the Flying C Ranch. He knew the Flying C owners were good people at heart, but he still faulted them for what they'd allowed to happen. Still, somehow, by the grace of God, he'd found a place in the middle of winter where he thought he might be able to truly fit in. That alone was enough to keep him awake. Eventually his mind would settle, but then he'd start thinking of the way David kept looking at him. Brian had had such a crush on him when he was in school. For him it hadn't been one of those admiration things. He'd dreamed of David when he was younger, and the football star had played a huge role in Brian's fantasy time behind the barn. And he'd had a very fertile imagination back then. Of course, like everything else, over time those feelings had faded.

Seeing him again, however, had brought back all those memories. There had never been anything between them; Brian had actually been shocked that David had remembered him at all. Not that it really mattered. He'd lost his last place largely because he'd gotten involved with one of the other men. He was sure David was gay, but unlike Rocklin at the Flying C, David wasn't so deep in the closet that he'd sell his soul and even make someone else's life miserable… or go as far as drive them off the place simply to keep his *deep, dark* secret.

Brian had been so stupid. He berated himself silently for what had to be the millionth time. He'd thought Rocklin cared, but of course all he'd ever been interested in was getting his rocks off. Well, at least Brian had gotten even just before he'd taken off. The bastard deserved it.

He rolled over on the clean, soft sheets and sighed. He needed to get some sleep. He fully intended to be a part of the ranch and prove he was someone worth keeping around. Brian wasn't sure how he would do that, but he intended to try. He tried to will his mind to stop whirling in circles and his body to relax. It did him no good at all.

The wind whistled outside the bedroom he was using. At one point he heard a soft click, and then the hum of the generator went silent. Footsteps sounded in the hall, and then the heat came on again, and this time it stayed. Phillip had turned it down because they were on generator power, but apparently the regular power had come back on.

"Everything is fine," he heard Phillip whisper, and then a door snicked closed.

Brian rolled over again and closed his eyes, taking a deep breath and doing his best to clear his mind. He was dog tired and worn out. He'd been through a hell of a lot in the past few days, and it was starting to catch up with him. He'd just begun to drift off when a soft moan reached his ears. He dismissed it until he heard it again.

"Oh God" came a soft whimper.

Brian's eyes popped open. He had a pretty good idea of what was going on in the other room. He didn't hear it again for a minute, and then it was back, louder and much more insistent. The last thing he wanted to hear was Haven and Phillip going at it. He remembered how Rocklin had been. They'd gone to a hotel once, well away from the ranch, and Rocklin had talked dirty the entire time they'd been there—a steady stream of filth. Brian had eventually put his hand over Rocklin's mouth to shut him up. He half expected to hear stuff like that, but there was nothing. Just the occasional moan or whimper making its way to his ears. Eventually it quieted, and Brian closed his eyes once again.

Now, of course, he was excited and thinking about sex. He groaned and thought about taking care of things on his own, but he was too tired, and his dick would go down on its own if he simply thought about something else. Eventually he fell asleep. He must have, because he jumped slightly at a sharp knock on his door. "Yeah, I'm up," Brian said and then yawned.

The door cracked open. "I'm going to get things started. The snow is really deep, and we're going to have to figure out how to give the cattle some room to move. They're getting stuck in the snow," Haven said.

"Okay. I'll get dressed and be right out." He glanced at the clock and realized he had been asleep, but only for a few hours. It was still fully dark outside, and the clock read just before six. Brian dressed and then hurried across the hall to the bathroom, where he shaved and got cleaned up as quickly as he could. He found Haven in the living room, talking quietly on the phone.

"At least the temperature seems to be breaking. It's already near freezing," Haven said. That meant if the sun did come out, it was going to be a heavy, sloppy mess in a few days, just like Haven had predicted. "We're going to put our heads together and figure something out. I'll talk to you later." Haven hung up and then began pulling on his gear. "I pulled out some things for you," he said, pointing to a thick coat, hat, and gloves on one of the chairs.

"Thanks," Brian said, and he began getting ready to go outside. "My boots are in the trunk of my car." He didn't go into the fact that he'd had to leave the Flying C in a hurry, so he'd thrown his things in the car with very little thought.

"I'll get them and be right back." Brian gave Haven the keys and continued getting ready. By the time Haven returned, Brian was ready to go. Haven handed Brian his old boots, and he pulled them on. Haven then handed him a plate and a mug of coffee. "You'll need to wolf it." Brian didn't need to be told twice, and then, when he was ready, he followed Haven outside. Most of the other men had already gathered just outside the barn.

"Are the horses set?" Haven asked.

"Gus and I got everything taken care of," David said.

"Good. Okay, guys, the problem is that we've had so much snow the herd can't really move. We got to give them a place where they can stand, and they're going to need a break from the wind."

"We already got them in the sheltered areas," one of the men said. "How can we do more? We can't melt the snow or stop it from coming down."

"Why don't we kill two birds with one stone?" Brian asked softly, and the others turned to him, slightly surprised. He was ready to just quiet down, but he plowed on, so to speak. "The land around here is really open for a long way. So if we need a windbreak, we'll have to make it ourselves. You have heavy equipment, right?" Brian turned to Haven, who nodded a little stiffly. "And the ground is frozen, so use the equipment to pile up the snow like they do in big city parking lots. Use it to create a berm. The pile will provide a windbreak, and the area you clear will give the cattle a place to stand without being up to their bellies. The only thing you have to be careful of is not to go too deep, because you don't want to tear up the grass underneath. Just move the snow."

"How do we get the equipment in and out?" Haven asked.

"We could use the same paths we do with the ATVs. They're sloped enough that we should be able to get it in," David suggested.

Haven thought for a few seconds. "All right, let's give it a try. But don't get the bucket loader stuck or we'll never get it out. And it's supposed to warm up today, so if we're going to try to do this, we need to start now, and if it starts to get soft, we gotta pull the equipment out fast. And for God's sake don't tear up my range," Haven growled. "Now let's get to work. We've got a herd to try to save and feed."

The men all gathered around him, and Brian explained his idea further. Since he didn't know the land, the men determined the best places to start clearing and piling the snow. They agreed to work in teams because the drivers would need direction and extra eyes to watch the herd.

Brian ended up on the team with David and a ranch hand named Hugh, and they all climbed into a tractor with a bucket on the front and headed out to one of the ranges. They had to dig a trail down and carefully open the gate. Then they began clearing a hundred-foot gap on the western edge, piling snow as high as they could. They worked methodically, slowly making their way across the land. Brian and David watched the herd, doing their best to keep them away from where they were working, but the cattle quickly found the areas where it was easier going and settled in the cleared area. It took hours to pile the snow, and then it took a long time to get the equipment back out. It was nearing noon before they got the bucket loader back out onto the road and closed the gate.

David called Haven. "It really seems to be working," he began, and Brian listened with a smile. "We need feed over here." David listened for a few seconds and then hung up. "Haven is sending a team of guys with a load of feed. He said we should head back. The sun is melting things enough that he wants the equipment off the land. He said one of the teams down at the other end of the ranch needs our help, so let's go." They climbed in the cab as best they could and set off.

Brian was crammed right next to David, while Hugh drove as quickly as he could. When they got to where they had been sent, they found one of the other loaders tilted slightly to the side, stuck about ten feet from the road.

"This area is usually wet and low. We thought it was frozen, but...," Mario said as soon as they got out. "We need to get it out as soon as possible. The sun is going to continue to warm up the air, and we could lose the loader if it rolls on its side."

"Okay," Brian said and began looking over the situation.

"We need to get it towed out," David said, and they got chains. The men began to attach the chains.

"No," Brian said. "Don't attach it there." He hurried over to where the others were working. "If you do, the pressure is going to pull it sideways and things will get worse." He looked things over carefully. "Hook it there to start with. We'll tug it upright and then a little this way to more solid ground. Then we can pull it out."

"Are you sure? I'm Mario, the foreman, by the way. You must be Brian, the new guy."

"It's good to meet you, and, yeah, I'm sure. It needs to get to solid ground first. Then we can drive and pull it out together. But if we try to just pull it out, it could tip, and then we're done."

Mario walked over to the equipment and looked around. Then he turned to one of the guys and said something Brian didn't hear, but he pointed to where they were originally going to attach the chain. The man attached it, and Brian knew he'd been overruled. He only hoped he was wrong. Brian looked to see if there was anyone he could appeal to, but Mario was the foreman, and Brian had offered his opinion and why. He was also the new guy, and his word didn't count for much.

"David, get in the cab and start the engine. When I wave my hand, put it in gear and we'll slowly pull you out," Mario said. Brian looked around, wondering why David was being put in the cab and realized the other men had already climbed up onto the roadbed and David was the closest man. Brian had heard there was a history between them, and he wondered if that had anything to do with it. Granted, it was most likely that David was simply closest.

They got into position, and Brian turned away. He couldn't look… and yet he ended up turning back around as the engines roared to life and the tractor they'd arrived in began to pull. Just like Brian had said, the center of gravity was off, and the stuck piece of equipment rocked and twisted, straightening up, but then as soon as it moved forward, it began to tilt again, this time farther. Everyone began to yell, and everything came to a stop.

David was still in the cab of the bucket loader, tilting away from the road. "Don't move at all," Brian yelled at the top of his lungs, springing into action. "No one move!" he screamed, and everything halted. Foreman or not, Brian glared at Mario. "If you keep pulling, it will go over, and if he tries to move too much, it'll go over."

Everyone looked at him. "Keep tension on the chain, don't let it go loose," he told the driver, his heart pounding as he saw the naked fear in David's expression. "Is there any rope?" he asked, and a hand raced to one of the trucks and brought over a coil. "Loop it around the bucket arm as high up as you can get," Brian said, and the man carefully made his way to the stranded piece of equipment. "That's it. Tie it off good, but don't put any pressure on the loader." Everyone around him held his breath as Brian watched the man tie a good knot and then another. "Excellent. Now, bring the other end up here."

He did as Brian asked. "Okay, here's what we have to do. Everyone is going to pull on this rope at the same time. We should have enough leverage to keep the loader upright. We only need to go a few more feet and the tires will hit solid ground. David, as soon as we begin pulling, put the loader in gear and very slowly inch forward." David nodded, and the men all grabbed the rope, including Mario.

"Okay, guys, pull," Mario called, and the loader shifted back the way they wanted it. Brian motioned, and the tractor began tugging. The loader moved forward, and Brian motioned them to continue.

"Pull harder, guys, all at once." They put their backs into it, and the loader lurched and then straightened. The tractor moved forward, and they released the rope as the loader reached solid ground and then came up onto the road. It was covered in mud, but out and in one piece. David opened the cab door and jumped down, then rushed over to where Brian waited.

"Damn, you were good," David said, clapping Brian on the back. "That was quick thinking."

"It sure was," Mario said a little sheepishly. "How'd you know to do that? And how did you know how it would behave?"

Brian shrugged and stepped back with a smile. "I just did. I've been pulling stuff out of mud for years, and I guess I learned it isn't as straightforward as it seems sometimes."

"Okay guys, let's get back," Mario called, and everyone piled into vehicles. Some peeled off into what Brian assumed was Dakota's driveway, while they continued on to Haven's. Everyone piled out of the trucks and equipment when they arrived. Haven had obviously been called, and he came out with a grin on his face.

"I heard you saved their bacon," Haven said.

"I was only trying to help," Brian explained. He kept his opinion to himself—that if Mario had listened to him in the first place, there wouldn't have been a need for any bacon saving. He simply smiled and nodded. Accolades weren't needed. But maybe now Haven would think about keeping him on more permanently.

"Go on in and get some lunch. I know everyone's hungry," Haven called, and the group trooped inside. Brian hung behind and noticed that David did the same.

"Why didn't Mario listen?" Brian asked once they were alone.

"He didn't know you and he thought he was right," David answered. "Mario is a good foreman and a decent man, but he tends to stick to his own counsel sometimes. I suppose if he knew you better, he would have done what you suggested up front, but…."

"He won't resent me, will he?" Brian asked.

"I doubt it. You were right, and Mario isn't one to hold grudges." David smiled. "I owe you a huge thank-you for your quick thinking. I was stuck in that loader, and if it had gone over…."

"It wasn't likely to keep rolling, but you never know." All Brian could see as the loader kept leaning was David being crushed under the piece of equipment. That was why he'd sprung into immediate action, regardless of the consequences.

"Well, you saved me. I thought the loader wasn't going to stop moving," David told him. "It felt like it would teeter over at any second."

"I know," Brian said as calmly as he could and then looked toward the house. "We better go inside if we want a chance at anything for lunch."

They headed indoors. There were two places at the table next to each other, and they both sat down. A plate of sandwiches sat in the center of the table. It had obviously been greatly diminished, but there were plenty left. Brian took one and began to eat. He was starved, and hadn't realized how long it had been since he'd last eaten until he took the first bite.

The conversation centered on him, as the guys told the story to the men who hadn't been there. Somehow the story kept getting bigger and bigger, with Mario being cast as the bad guy.

"That's not true. Mario didn't say anything like that to me," Brian said when one of the men claimed Mario had told Brian to get back to work. "He made his decision, and I'm just glad I was there to help get David out. That's all there is to it."

Gus and some of the other men nodded, and thankfully the conversation turned to the weather. Apparently another storm was predicted in a few days. Haven discussed what he thought they could expect and his plans to help the ranch prepare for it.

"In the meantime, let's make sure all the stocks and stores are replenished. We need to make sure there's firewood for both us and up at Dakota and Wally's," Haven said. "The herds must get feed and plenty of it. If they get too stressed, we'll start to lose them. Today and tomorrow are a reprieve and a chance to catch up. We have to make the most of it." Haven turned to David. "Get some of the men later this afternoon and make sure all the horses are exercised. They've been in the barn for days and they'll need a good outing. Plows should be out on the roads, so you might want to take some of the horses for a ride. Today and tomorrow are probably all we'll have before we get another bout of this."

"You got it," David said, and Brian shared a look with him. He very much wanted to go for a ride. It had been too long since he'd spent time on a horse, and a ride would be just the ticket. Of course, that depended on what other things Haven wanted him to do. "Brian can help me this afternoon."

Haven nodded and his gaze traveled around the table as he handed out assignments. Phillip agreed to help with the horses. He was a decent rider and could help with exercising and grooming. Ten minutes later, lunch broke up and everyone left the house to get to work.

BRIAN SPENT the afternoon cleaning out stalls and then grooming horses, working alongside David. He had soon stripped off his coat and was working in his shirt and sweatshirt, generating heat of his own as he shoveled the soiled stall bedding. He filled the wheelbarrow and headed out to the muck pile, passing David as he went. He'd taken off his coat as well, and Brian couldn't help sneaking a peek at him as he passed.

Brian paused and gasped a little once David approached the door. He had never been able to resist a cowboy encased in a pair of jeans that seemed one size too small. When David turned the corner, Brian went back to what he was doing.

He wasn't going to get involved with anyone at work, he knew that, but looking certainly wouldn't hurt, and damned if David wasn't still really fine to look at. He wasn't big or bulky, but he filled out the chest and arms of his shirt nicely with a body chiseled from hard work. In high school, Brian had been small, but years of work had given him the same kind of body. Granted, his wasn't as fine as the one he imagined beneath David's clothes. He was still wiry and on the small side—thin, some people would say. Brian passed David, smiling as David returned and he made his way out. The horses being inside for days meant they had really dirtied the stalls, and there was a lot to do, so Brian kept moving, putting down fresh bedding and then shifting horses until they were all in their fresh stalls, brushed, and happily munching away.

"Are you ready to go for a ride?" Phillip asked as he strode into the barn. There was still some daylight left. David pointed out which horses to saddle, and they got busy. Since the horses were brushed already, they just needed to saddle them and then get back into their coats and hats.

"It doesn't have to be too long. As cold as it is, the horses just need to walk. No trotting or running. This is just for them to stretch their legs, and then we'll get another set of three. So fifteen, twenty minutes ought to be enough, and be sure to watch for ice. We don't want anyone to fall."

Brian knew all that, and Phillip was nodding as well. They mounted. David took the lead, with Phillip in the rear. As they rode, it didn't take Brian very long to lock on to the view in front of him or to remember how difficult it was to ride with a hard-on. David was really fine looking normally, but gorgeous in the saddle, his butt bouncing slightly. Brian appreciated a high, tight cowboy butt, and this was a particularly stellar example.

Brian heard Phillip speed up his horse until he was riding next to him. "What are you watching so intently?" Phillip winked at him, and Brian knew his cover had been blown.

"Nothing," he whispered. "Just watching the area ahead for slick spots," he added more loudly. "We really need to be careful." The only spot they could ride in relative safety was by the side of the road, where it had been plowed. Thankfully, there weren't many cars and they could see and be seen for quite a distance. "They sure like being out, don't they?" Brian's horse tossed his head as if he understood him.

"They hate being cooped up as much as we do," David called back and pulled to a stop. "We'd best head back. We can take them out again tomorrow, but if we don't keep moving, there won't be time to exercise the others. Besides, as the sun goes down, the temperature is going to drop, and that won't be good for any of us."

They turned around, and David led them back. Brian still watched him, but had to do it in such a way that Eagle-Eye Phillip didn't call him out on it again. When they reached the yard, they unsaddled the horses and got them settled in their stalls, then saddled another three and took them for the same relatively short ride. By the time they returned, the sun was getting low in the sky and the temperature had already begun to fall.

"Go on in. We'll take care of things here," Brian told Phillip.

"Thanks, I promised Haven I'd help with dinner. After everything everyone did today, he's making something special. So don't be too late." Phillip hurried away, and Brian wondered just what kind of dinner was being served. Or maybe it was the prospect of an appetizer that had Phillip so excited. Brian reminded himself to knock and make plenty of noise when he went into the house.

He unsaddled his horse and then Phillip's, brushed them both down quickly, and put the tack away. He'd just set the last saddle in place when he saw David leaning against the doorframe, watching him. Brian warmed instantly and felt David's gaze travel over him. He didn't move for a few seconds, waiting to see what David would do.

"Guys, are you ready for dinner?" Phillip called, his voice echoing through the barn.

"Yeah. We're done here and we'll be right in," Brian called back and walked toward the doorway, the spell broken. He wasn't going to get involved, and he wasn't going to have a quick fling with anyone on the ranch, he reminded himself, even as he got close enough to David to get a noseful of eau de cowboy, and damned if it wasn't thick and heady in the extreme. He actually blinked a few times and forced himself to keep going. Anything he did other than walk away would not end well. He'd learned that already, and he had just gotten the job here. He couldn't jeopardize that for anything. "Are you coming to eat?" he managed to ask without his voice breaking like a teenager's.

"You bet," David said softly and followed him toward the barn door.

They headed inside and Brian was instantly assaulted by the most amazing scent ever. Aromas of roast beef and spices filled the entire place, along with roasted potatoes. Brian's mouth watered instantly and he tried to remember the last time he'd had a meal like that. It had to be the last Christmas he was home. His mother always cooked like that for the holidays. The olfactory memory nearly transported him home... almost. He stopped himself before making the imaginary trip. That was one road he really didn't need to go down, at least not now.

"Take off your coats and stuff," Phillip said. "You know where they go."

"Are we celebrating?" David asked.

"Sort of. The weather forecast says it'll be in the forties by the end of the week. That should give all of us a break from this cold and snow. We've got the cattle so they can move around, and thanks to Brian, here, we don't have a piece of equipment lying on its side in one of the ranges... so let's think of it as a well-deserved reward for all of us."

More people began arriving, including Dakota, who introduced Brian to Wally. Dakota asked to take a look at his feet, so Brian led him to the room he was using, and Dakota checked him over.

"They look good, and you were very lucky. You're going to have to keep them extra warm for a while. Both your hands and feet will be susceptible to the cold for some time."

"But I thought they looked good," Brian said as he started putting on his socks.

Dakota stood back up. "They do. But they were still damaged and will need time to heal. So be careful and be sure to call if they feel numb," Dakota told him.

Brian agreed and finished putting on his socks and boots. They rejoined the group, which had gotten even larger. The entire ranch must have been invited. Brian helped David set up tables and chairs in the living room, and soon the meat was out of the oven and the food set up on the kitchen counter. Everyone lined up and took turns filling their plates. Brian hung back a little.

"If you wait, you won't get nothing," Gus said from behind him, so Brian got in line.

He sat at a small table with Mario, Gus, and Gordon, who was introduced as Mario's partner. "Were you a Marine?" Brian asked. "You have the look."

"I was in the Corps," Gordon said. "I've been here on the ranch for a little over six months." Gordon lightly bumped Mario's shoulder and then caught Mario's eyes.

"I should have listened to you today," Mario said softly and then took a bite of his roast.

"It all worked out, and that's what counts," Brian replied as graciously as he could. "I'm glad I could help."

"Where did you learn about things like that? I mean, you knew what it would do," Mario said, putting down his fork. "Are you an engineer or something?"

"No. I wanted to go to school for architecture, but it wasn't in the cards." Brian paused a second. "I guess I could just imagine what would happen and sort of saw it in my mind. I've always been able to do that."

"It was also his idea to use the snow as a windbreak," David said, leaning back slightly from the table next to theirs.

"So we have you to thank for all this," Gordon said. At first Brian wasn't sure how to take it, but Gordon smiled and winked once. "I'm kidding. It was a great idea and will really give the cattle a break from the wind."

Most of the dinner conversation revolved around ranch issues. Wally told him and David that he would be over in the morning to check over the horses. He was concerned about the amount of time they had been spending in their stalls. He was pleased they were getting exercise, but wanted to confirm there were no issues. "We're spot cleaning the stalls daily," David said.

Wally chuckled a little. "I'm not disparaging the care you're giving them. I just want to be sure to head off any problems. I know you had them out today and plan to do the same tomorrow, but then they'll be cooped up again." Wally patted David on the shoulder, and Brian's stomach tightened a little. He hated that Wally was touching David. He wanted to be the one to touch David like that. "I looked at the horses in our barn today."

"How are the cats taking this cold?" Brian asked. He'd been dying to see them.

"They're not doing too badly. I have to feed them a ton and make sure they have bedding to curl up in. They have covered shelters they can retreat to, and as long as they're out of the wind and can build a den that they can heat with their bodies, they're fine."

"You made little cat houses," Dakota said loudly, and all the guys chuckled.

"Very funny," Wally said. "Actually, it was Liam who made the houses. Although I will say the cats do better in warm weather than cold, so I'll be happy once these extreme temperatures are behind us."

"How do you control the snow? If they're in cages, then they can fill up, and it isn't like the cats will let you in to shovel," Brian said.

"We cover parts of the enclosures with plywood and tie it down. It limits the snow that can get in. You should come by. Liam and I could show you what we've done."

Brian grinned. "That would be so cool. I saw pictures of you and the lion who liked to have his belly scratched."

"He was special. Unfortunately, I didn't have him for very long. Schian was old when I got him, and he stayed with us only for a year or so. Then he passed away. I miss him—he was like a big housecat. I never let anyone else get close to him, because I didn't know how he would react, but for me, he was like a pet. I always respected him, though. Even old and on his back, he had claws and teeth and could do a lot of damage if he decided to. But mostly he was a big baby."

Most people had finished eating and began shifting around. Brian made room, and Wally came over and joined their table to make it easier to continue the conversation. "So what was the hardest animal you've had? I mean, which one was hardest to care for?"

"Shahrazad," a bunch of the guys said at the same time.

"Yeah. She was a Bengal tiger, very valuable and mean as they came. She hadn't been treated well, and I think she equated all humans with those who'd hurt her. It took a while, but she did eventually calm down so that Liam or I could care for her. But I never went into her enclosure while she was there. That would have been suicide. She's at a zoo now, and the keepers tell me she's doing really well. She's had at least one litter of cubs, and is by all accounts a great mother." Wally paused. "You should come over, and we'll show you around. Right now I have eleven cats, with room for one more. Hopefully in the spring I'll be able to place a few more of them. My goal is to make sure they're healthy. The older ones get a place to retire, and the younger ones I nurse back to health and try to place in zoos."

"That's really cool. How do you pay for them? I mean, it must cost a lot to feed and house them."

"It does," Wally said. "But I love them, so it's what I do." Dakota came over and placed his hands on Wally's shoulders, standing behind him, quietly offering comfort. "Sometimes people actually buy exotic cat cubs and think they're pets, until they get larger and become more than they can handle."

"A few months ago, Wally got a call from a family in Rapid City. They had done just that. Now it's illegal, but the real problem is that the animal often gets abused, or worse…. Anyway, Wally rushed over and brought back a two-month-old tiger cub. The poor thing…."

"Is it one of the eleven?" Brian asked, and Wally shook his head.

"I couldn't save him. He had gotten so aggressive that they had locked him in a room in their basement, and while they had tried to feed him, he still needed care and had been removed from his mother too soon."

"What happened?" Brian whispered.

"I called the police and let them deal with it. Those people never should have had the cub in the first place. It was so sad. I've had people contact me about buying cubs and all kinds of things." Wally shook his head.

"Have you ever thought about having any of them stuffed after they died?" As soon as Brian asked the question, he knew the answer and was afraid he shouldn't have asked, but Wally didn't get angry.

"No. Once they die, I have a place on the property where I bury them. There's a big cat graveyard, away from where I keep them. Their pelts are very valuable, and I've thought about skinning them before burial, but I can't bring myself to do it. So I bury them intact and with as much care as I show them when they're alive." It was clear to Brian that Wally's cats held a special place in his heart. They might not have been the kind of animal that curled in his lap and purred, but he obviously had a bond with them that continued even after they were gone. "Did you have pets growing up?"

"Yes and no," Brian answered, and Wally leaned on the table. "The ranch had dogs, of course, and there was one I was really close to. His name was Skipper, and he went everywhere I did from the time I was about nine years old. But he was one of the ranch dogs. My dad was the foreman. Anyway, Skipper died when I was about fourteen, and I asked my dad for a dog of my own, but he said no. We lived on the property, and the owner of the ranch was getting older and they weren't replacing any of the pets. He said I was going to be leaving home in a few years and that he and Mom would end up caring for the dog, so that was it."

"That sucks," David said. "I had a collie growing up. His name was Trooper and he would try to herd anything. When me and my friends were playing outside, he'd herd us into the center of the yard. I loved that dog." David chuckled, and Brian loved the warm expression on his face. "He was gray and white with a pink nose. One of my friends said he looked like a giant guinea pig, but he was my best friend." David turned to him. "I can't imagine growing up without him."

Brian nodded. He'd wanted a dog of his own more than anything. But he'd always had to make do with one of the ranch dogs. And they were never his. Someone else decided what happened to them. But after he left home, it hadn't mattered so much.

Some of the guys began to say their good-nights and filter outside. He heard a group of them making plans to go into town for the evening.

"There's plenty to be done tomorrow, so don't think about getting wasted, because anyone with a hangover will certainly be spending the day working around the loudest piece of equipment I can find," Haven said.

Brian stifled a laugh as he saw some of the guys' faces. Haven was serious, and they all seemed to know it. Brian thought it sounded like an excellent deterrent for overindulgence. They filed out, and the house quieted. Conversations wound down as people got ready to leave for the evening. Brian needed something to do, so he went into the kitchen and helped with the dishes.

When the dishes were done, he and Phillip came back into the living room. Wally, Dakota, David, Haven, Mario, and Gordon were sitting around one of the tables, playing poker.

"You could have waited," Phillip said.

Haven chuckled, throwing a few chips in the center of the table. "I call." Then he looked up at Phillip. "You know you don't like to play."

"I do too," Phillip said. "I just always lose." Phillip leaned over the table and swiped a stack of Haven's chips. "And because of that crack, I'm going to play with your money tonight." Phillip sat down, and Haven groaned. Brian sat back and watched. He didn't have much cash and he wasn't going to risk it playing cards. Haven invited him to play, but poker had never really been his game. As they continued to bet, though, he realized they weren't playing for much, and eventually he got out his wallet and pulled out a five to get some chips.

"Do you play often?" Brian asked as Haven dealt the cards.

"More in the winter than the summer. When things slow down, we can get together a little more," Dakota explained. They looked at their cards and bet around the table.

Brian schooled his expression carefully and bet. He had good cards that kept getting better and better. He ended up winning the first pot.

"So what's on the agenda for tomorrow?" he asked Haven.

"All the usual stuff, plus more preparations for the next storm. The weather reports keep fluctuating, so we could get another foot of snow or nothing at all, depending on the track of the storm. It's always like this, except this year it seems like we get hit with it every single time, so I want to make sure we're ready."

They played for a few hours, until it started getting late. Everyone around the table was an early riser, so they called it a night and cashed in their winnings. Brian had done very well and ended up with the largest share of the money. Granted, it was only an extra fifteen dollars, but it felt good.

He and David helped clean up and put everything away. Then David said good night and left. Brian went to the guest room and got ready for bed. Tomorrow he was planning to move into the room in the bunkhouse, which was a bit of a relief when he heard the soft moans beginning. He put them out of his mind as best he could and tried to get some sleep.

THE FOLLOWING day, Brian helped in the barn and moved into the bunkhouse. He also worked a lot with the horses and did whatever else he was asked to do. It felt nice to have a place where he seemed to belong, and by the end of the day he was exhausted and fell right to sleep. He woke the following day to yelling.

"We got fences down." It was Haven, and everyone jumped to it.

Brian pulled on his clothes and was out in the yard before he could even think about it.

"What happened?" he asked David when he saw him. Men were already climbing into trucks, and he followed suit.

"It happens. The cattle trampled some of the fence because it was buried in the snow, and once it was down, the stupid things went on through. It isn't like there's anything more to eat on the outside of the fence than inside," David explained. "We're going to help find the head that are loose while the others figure out how to repair what got damaged." They rode out to the break, and in the early morning light, Brian could easily see the trail through the snow where the cattle had broken through. Where they'd gone was no great secret, but it was going to be the devil trying to follow them.

"Okay. Stay in pairs and work your way to the strays. We'll get the fence repaired to keep any others from joining them," Haven said. "Make sure you have a phone and stay in touch." Haven looked upward. "There'll be more snow in a few hours. If you're out and it starts, hightail it back here. We'll find whatever head are left after it's over." Brian knew that really meant that whatever cattle they didn't find probably wouldn't be worth finding. The herd stayed alive in weather like this by sharing warmth and eating the feed they were provided. There wasn't anything to forage for in the snow, and alone in the middle of a blizzard, a lone head wouldn't last very long. Ranches existed and profited by making the most they could off each head in the herd. Losses, even small ones, could add up to a lot and affect the ranch's viability. Brian knew that. He'd lived through it once, and he never wanted to do it again.

He jumped down from the truck and made sure he was well braced against the cold before following David off through the snow on the trail of what he hoped was a small piece of the herd. "Do you think we'll find them?" he asked as they trudged along. The cattle had cut a path, so it was easier going than it would have been otherwise, but still difficult. In places, the snow was still well over their knees, making each step difficult.

"Yeah, but we don't have much time. The clouds keep getting lower and lower," David said. Thankfully, the air had been still.

"I know," Brian said and began moving faster. "Do you hear that?" he said a few minutes later, and they both stopped.

"Yeah, something is over here," David said. They pushed ahead quickly and got to a small rise. They descended the other side and followed the sound down a little ways. A few bare trunks of small trees and shrubs stuck out of the snow. They continued following the trail until they saw movement ahead.

A small group of cattle stood at the base of the ravine. They moved and stomped down the snow, probably trying to get to the bottom of it so they could find something to eat. "Let's work our way around the other side so we can try to get them moving back the way they came," David suggested, and Brian nodded.

"Call Haven and let him know what we found," Brian said. David pulled out his cell phone and dialed, and Brian stood there, waiting for it to connect. David looked at the phone and began pressing buttons again.

"Try yours. I'm not getting much of a signal, and it won't connect."

"I don't have one," Brian told him. Being broke as shit was not conducive to having cell phones or much else. "I could try to go back and see if I can get a better signal someplace else."

"No. Let's see if we can get these bastards moving back toward the ranch. We can call Haven as soon as we're on our way." David signaled, and they began making a large circle around the group of cattle. It was hard going, breaking their own trail, and Brian kept glancing at the sky every few minutes, expecting snow to begin any second.

"Jesus, my legs feel like lead," David mumbled as they got to the far side.

"Yeah," Brian said, "mine too." Thankfully, he'd prepared for this as soon as he'd been told what happened, and he'd put on extra socks and overdressed for the cold. So while tired, he was warm enough. But all that could change and he knew it. "Let's get them the hell out of here," he yelled as soon as they got to the back side. David yelled too, and then the cattle startled and began moving. He and David followed, continuing to make as much noise as possible.

He moved as quickly as he could and made it to where the cattle had packed down the snow. The going got easier then, and Brian took off behind the small group of steers, yelling to keep them moving. Brian knew that, now the steers were on the move, they were likely to follow their own path right back home. Veering off would only slow them, and once the other men saw them coming, they would take over and get them with the rest of the herd. "David, try calling Haven now. They're well on their way!" Brian turned around but didn't see David anywhere. "Shit!" He raced back the way he'd come, calling for David and then listening.

"Brian," he heard just ahead and off to the side. Brian found David just off the path and raced up to the spot of blue.

"What happened?" Brian asked as he approached.

"I stepped off the path and there was stuff under the snow. I twisted my ankle," David said.

"Can you walk?' Brian asked and tried to help David to his feet.

"I don't think so, but I'll try." David got to his feet, and Brian put David's arm over his shoulder and helped stabilize his left side. David took a tentative step, and they made it out onto the path before David lost his balance and fell. "It hurts like bloody hell."

"Okay. Try to get a signal on the phone and call Haven. They have to have some way to get out here."

David felt around the pockets of his pants and then coat, moving a little more frantically. "I don't have it. Fuck." He checked his pockets again. "It must have fallen out when I slipped."

Brian went back to where he'd found David and looked around. He didn't see the phone anywhere and began sifting through the snow, with no luck. "I can't find it," he said. Then something glinted at his feet. He reached into the snow and came up with the phone. "I found it," he cried with jubilation and rubbed off the snow before pulling off a glove and stared at the blank screen. He tried turning it on and nothing happened. He headed back to where David rested in the snow and handed it to him.

David tried as well and shook his head. "It's dead. I had plenty of charge when we left. It must have been warm enough that some moisture got in it when it was in the snow." He shook it violently and tried again. Of course nothing happened.

"Okay. The cattle were headed back their way. When they show up and we don't, they'll send people out looking. Either that or we can try again." As Brian said those words, the first flakes of snow began to fall.

"Let's try," David said, and Brian helped him up.

They made it about four steps, with David gritting his teeth and hissing the entire time. Brian could tell they were going to get nowhere, and stopped. The snow was falling more heavily and the air that had been still began to move, slowly at first, but then more steadily.

"You need to go back and try to get help. You can make it," David said.

Brian was about to do as David said, but the snow got heavier, and with the wind, he realized that yes, he might get back to the ranch, but it was unlikely he'd be able to find David again. The wind would obliterate the trail, and David would get colder and colder while they looked for him. He wasn't going to let anything happen to David, and he wasn't leaving.

The snow started to come down harder, and Brian looked around and then turned to David. "We need to get out of the wind. Did you ever make a snow fort when you were a kid?" he asked.

"Of course."

"Then make one now. Pile the snow up all around you. We need to dig a place big enough for the two of us, and we need to get as close to the ground as possible. Use this spot as a starting point. The cattle cleared most of the snow. We can use the snow you remove as a windbreak."

"What are you going to do?" David asked him as he settled on the snow and began to dig.

"I'm going to see if there's any dead wood I can use to start a fire," Brian explained. "I keep a small kit in my pocket. There are a few matches and some floss that will catch and burn easily. But I need to find some wood, and since the wind is most likely going to pick up, we're going to need shelter of some kind." Brian turned and walked toward the scrub and brush. There were a few evergreen trees mixed in, with dead branches at the base. Brian broke them off and created a pile of branches. He knew these were so full of pitch that they would catch easily and increase their chances of getting the fire started. Then he got lucky and located a few branches sticking out of the snow. He pulled and got some larger branches. He hauled them back to where David was working. He'd created an indentation in the snow that was about eighteen inches deep, the ground just beginning to show. Brian broke off a branch and handed it to David. "Use this if you need to."

"Okay," David said, taking it.

"Do you happen to have a knife, any kind of knife?" Brian asked, and David patted his pockets, then pulled out a small Swiss Army knife. He handed it to Brian.

"Thanks," Brian said and hurried away again. The wind was steadily picking up and so was the snow. It was going to be a blizzard soon enough, and he still had a lot to do. He used the knife to cut small, live branches from the evergreens and began hauling back armload after armload. He nearly stripped one of the trees bare, but he continued to work. He found more wood, and after digging down, pulled a few larger branches that must have been part of the scrubby trees nearby. He continued hauling it all back to near where David had piled and packed the snow.

"What's all that for?" David asked, pointing to the green branches.

"I'll show you in a few minutes. Let's get a fire started. Making it through any amount of time depends on it. By now, even if they've figured out we're missing, they aren't going to be able to send people to find us. The visibility is crap and getting worse."

"But it's still morning," David said. "Haven will find us."

"What if he can't?" Brian countered. "You have a sprained ankle and can't make it back. We need to keep warm as best we can to give them time to find us." Brian began to break up the pine sticks into small pieces, and then started on some of the others. He piled them at the far side of the cleared area. Then he pulled a small metal container about the size of a film canister out of his coat pocket and handed it to David. "Don't spill the matches. They're all we have." He made a platform on the ground with the sticks and then built a nest of even smaller sticks underneath. He placed the floss in the center and put more tiny twigs on top. There was plenty to catch. "Lean close. We need to block as much of the wind as we can."

The two of them pressed together, and Brian flicked one of the matches with his thumbnail. It flared to life and he lit the small bit of cotton. He got a small flame, which quickly caught on the pitchy pine and crackled softly. Brian added some more, feeding the twigs in one at a time. "I was a Boy Scout when I was a kid. I hated it because the other kids were such dicks, but thankfully there were a few lessons that stuck with me." He added a few bigger pieces of wood, and the flames got larger. Their windbreak seemed to be largely doing the trick, thank goodness.

He continued feeding in more wood, and the fire got hotter and more secure. He closed the small container and placed it back in his pocket. Then he added some large sticks, encircling the flame and heat in fuel, adding more and more kindling on top. "Okay, we have warmth, but I need to get some more wood because we'll burn through what I have pretty quickly. Just keep feeding the wood onto it and we'll be fine."

"What about all that?" David asked, pointing at the pine branches.

"We're going to rest here," Brian explained and motioned to the area right up against where the snow had been piled. "Line that with the branches. It will give us some insulation from the snow and ice. Just not too close to the fire." Brian stood up and stepped out of the shelter. The wind immediately went through him. "I'll be back as quickly as I can." He passed the wood he had found down to David and then hurried off.

Brian got lucky. After searching for a while, he found another branch that had a larger end. Parts of it were too big for him to break, but they could burn it in pieces. At least it was big enough to burn for more than a few minutes. He hauled back what he'd found and broke it up as best he could. The wood was wet, so he placed some of it near the fire to dry. David had spread out the evergreen branches, and Brian set the rest of them in the snow above them to provide some relief from what was still falling and blowing around.

He was cold now and carefully climbed into the shelter, built up the fire, and did his best to warm his hands and feet. The wind blew the flames around a little, but their shelter was surprisingly comfortable. They were out of the wind, they had a source of heat, and they were fairly dry. Now if he had pockets full of food, things would be nearly perfect. "How is your ankle?"

"It hurts like hell," David said. "I should be icing it, but out here that seems a little redundant. Are your feet and hands okay?"

"Yeah. They're a little tingly, but feeling better now that they can get warm again." He pulled off his gloves and placed his hands close to the warm fire. He was purposely not letting the fire get too large; otherwise, they would burn through the wood he'd gathered too quickly. And it would melt their shelter, which would leave them wet and only hasten the ability of the cold to seep into them.

Brian moved closer to David and held him.

"What are you doing?" David asked.

"Conserving heat. The fire is only going to do so much." Brian reached over and set the one end of the large branch carefully on the flames. It took a few minutes, but it caught, and the fire began burning a little hotter. His front half was warm enough, but the cold was starting to seep in through his back and bottom. The wind was blowing full-on now, and snow was coming down heavily. He needed a chance to warm up before he went back to try to find more branches and wood to burn. They had some time as long as they didn't burn through the wood too quickly. Brian shifted, and David tugged him closer.

"You could have left me and gone back," David whispered, his breath warm on Brian's ear.

"Yeah, but then you'd be out here alone, waiting for someone to find you. The trail we followed is being blown away by the minute." The wind came up, whipping around and above them. The fire danced and the flames waved, but they were protected enough that the wind largely left them alone. What worried Brian was the way the cold seeped through him. He scooted closer to the fire, and David moved closer to him.

Along with the wind, Brian could feel the temperature dropping. He'd taken off his gloves to warm his hands around the fire, but now he pulled them back on and soaked in as much warmth as he could. At least this time when he was stuck in the cold, he had a source of warmth. "How are you holding up?" he asked David quietly.

"I'm okay. The branches were a great idea. It would be nicer if we had something to put over us."

"I know." Brian was trying to figure out how to block more of the wind, but all the ideas he had involved leaving the protected area, and he wasn't sure he should do that yet. He needed to get warm, and while he was starting to feel the heat, he was still cold. Brian sniffled. His chest felt tight and he shivered again. He wondered if he was getting sick and hoped to hell he wasn't. He'd need all his strength to get through this—to get both of them through this. Brian took stock of what they had and figured there was enough wood for a few hours. Once half of it was gone, he'd have to get out and hunt for more.

David tugged at the zipper on the front of Brian's coat and then pulled down his own. Then he pulled them together, hugging Brian close and wrapping their coats around him. Warmth enclosed him, and when David slid his hands around his back and slowly rubbed up and down, the warmth he'd been missing settled in. Brian did the same for David. They needed to stay warm and they needed to remain focused, but David's scent and warmth surrounded him, and each time he took a breath, he inhaled his rich, musky scent. Brian closed his eyes and tried to think about where they were and what they should be doing. But then David shifted slightly and kissed him.

Without thinking twice, Brian kissed him back. Warmth spread though him from head to toe, and suddenly there was no wind, no snow—only heat, warmth, and David. The heat was followed by excitement, and he shifted, pressing David back. David started slightly, and Brian remembered where they were and what kind of danger they were in. He pulled away for a few seconds, but David drew him back in and kissed him hard. Brian moaned softly, but the sound was largely carried away by the wind. Not that it mattered. Who would have thought that out in the cold, hunkered down in a shelter, he could find such warmth and happiness? As long as David held him like this, he didn't care if they were found.

Brian moved away from David just long enough to shift the wood on the fire, then settled once again into David's warmth, resting his head on his shoulder. They didn't talk much; there was no need. The warmth between them said all he needed to hear.

"I used to watch you in high school," David whispered. "You had those long, floppy curls that fell into your eyes."

Brian stilled for a few seconds. He found it hard to believe anyone had noticed him. He'd been pretty good at disappearing.

"We were in geography class together," David continued. The wind whipped, and Brian turned as the flames dimmed and then flared back to life as soon as the gust died down. If this kept up, the wind would eventually snuff out the fire unless he built it hotter, but that meant the wood he'd gathered would last a lot less time. He carefully put another piece of wood on the fire, this one smaller, and it quickly flared to heat. He added a few more, and the warmth from the fire added to what David was sharing.

"I'm going to have to look for more wood soon," Brian said.

"I wish I could help," David said, and Brian nodded. David lightly brushed his cheek after pulling off a leather glove. "I really do remember you."

"Why would you have remembered me? You were the star. Everyone knew you, and you were the center of attention. I was the quiet kid who sat in the back of class and stayed to himself."

"Maybe," David told him. "But there was something about you. I kept looking at you when we were in class, and when we'd pass in the hall I had to stop my gaze from following you. I don't want to say that I knew you were like me, because I didn't really understand who I was back then. But maybe on some level I did. I don't know. But I remember how you used to sit in the corner of the cafeteria with that group of guys. You'd talk so earnestly about things, waving your hands like what you had to say was the most important thing in the world. At lunch I sat with the cheerleaders and football players, and all the girls talked about was their hair and who they hated because 'she thinks she's prettier.' The guys were no better, talking about who they got how far with and worrying about who was going to make what what team."

Brian chuckled lightly. "If I remember right, those conversations were over such important things as which *Star Trek* episode was more interesting or prophetic than the others. We were stupid, nerdy kids. We watched television and spent our lunch hours arguing over some stupid point. But we thought it was especially important at the time." Thankfully, David laughed along with him. "Maybe we weren't that different. We were growing up, trying to figure things out, and thinking we were alone in the world—that no one else was like us."

"And if you'd known? If we'd known... about each other?" David asked. "Would that have made things better?"

"I don't think so," Brian admitted. It seemed weird to be having this conversation now, with David's arms around him, but they'd both gone down this path, and Brian would be damned if he was going to pull away. "If I had admitted to you in high school that I was gay, would you have said you were too? Or would you have made fun of me and tried to make my life hell to cover up who you were?" Brian looked into David's eyes and then turned toward the fire. "You really don't have to answer, because I already know. You had way too much to lose back then, and all I wanted was to remain as invisible as possible."

"You don't know that," David countered.

"Yes, I do. Just like if you'd told me you were gay, I probably would have clammed up and stayed as far away from you as possible. High school was a crappy time. It wouldn't have mattered that you'd been starring in my late-night fantasies for months or that I'd invented an excuse to see the coach just so I could be in the locker room when you were changing clothes after practice a few times. I was as scared as a baby bird then. But I'm not now. At least I'm not as scared about being gay." That wasn't fully truthful, but he didn't want to go into all that now. Being gay basically sucked for him, and not in a good way. "Just like people finding out I was gay lost me the place I thought had been home for three years. The people there didn't think about the good work I'd done or how much I'd helped each of them. All they cared about was that I was gay and liked guys instead of girls. I have no idea what they expected I was going to do—start jumping them in the barn or something?" Brian began to shake, but it wasn't from the cold. David held him a little tighter. "Being gay has brought me almost nothing but pain."

"It doesn't have to be like that. Look at Haven and Phillip, or Dakota and Wally. There are other couples as well. Liam works for Wally, and he has a great partner." David smiled, and Brian wondered what was up. "If you go the other way from Dakota's, just a few miles is another ranch. That place is Willie Meadows's ranch. Once a year, the ranch throws a big party, and Willie and his partner always come. He sings a few songs and hangs out with everybody. He's a big star and he's gay. From the few times I've met him, he seems like a pretty good guy too."

"It's safe here," Brian said.

"No. It's just *safer* here. Dakota and Haven try to keep it that way, but no place is perfect. It can't be. There are people in town who try to cause trouble sometimes, and the sheriff isn't the most understanding guy from what I've seen, but it's good here. And you can be yourself."

"Yeah. I wish I knew who that was," Brian mumbled, and David didn't argue. He simply lightly nuzzled Brian's cheek, and when Brian turned away from the fire, David kissed him.

Damn, it felt good. David tasted like the out-of-doors—rich and clean. Brian returned the kiss with a passion that welled from deep inside him, passion and energy he didn't think he had in him still. He had figured those things had been squeezed out of him a long time ago. But they were there, and apparently they'd just been waiting for someone to awaken them. Brian had to shift slightly because he was hard and throbbing under multiple layers of clothing. He was pretty sure everything was stuffed tight enough that David couldn't tell. But then he smiled when he realized it hardly mattered, if what he was feeling against his belly was what he thought it was.

When David broke the kiss, Brian grinned and clung to him until the fire crackled. They broke apart long enough for Brian to add some more wood. As much as he didn't want to leave the shelter they'd built, he would need to get more wood soon or they would start running low. The snow was still coming down, and without plenty of wood that had had a chance to dry, they wouldn't be able to sustain the fire and they'd lose their only source of heat.

"I keep hoping that someone will figure out we're missing and come looking for us," David whispered.

"I know. It's nice in a rustic sort of way, but I think I'd rather be curled up on a sofa in front of the fire in the living room or something. Every time the wind blows, I expect it to blow out the fire, and then it would just be a matter of time," Brian said.

"Yeah. I suppose having a stocked kitchen at our disposal would help as well."

Brian hadn't had a chance to eat anything before they headed out, and he suspected David hadn't either. He was getting thirsty as well. The cold air was drying, but eating snow was not a particularly good thing to do. The snow would melt and provide water, but it would also lower the internal temperature of the body and hasten the effects of the cold. No, best to wait until help arrived. It had to come eventually. "I'll go out and get some wood in a few minutes."

Brian added a little more to the fire and pulled off his gloves to warm his hands thoroughly. Then he put them back on and zipped up his coat, making sure he was as bundled up as he could get.

As soon as he stood up, the wind caught him like a sail, trying to blow him over. He stepped out of the shelter and made his way across the drifting snow toward the wooded area. It was hard to see and he did his best to keep his back to the wind. He found some dead branches sticking out of the snow and made a pile of them. They weren't terribly big, but it was what he could find. He filled his arms and carried the wood back to the shelter, where he broke them into pieces and then handed them to David. Then he went back for more.

By the time he'd brought a second armload, his hands were cold and his back ached. He broke up the sticks and then climbed back into the shelter. David immediately moved closer to him, opened his coat, and pressed his chest to Brian's. The fire was going well and the wood he'd gathered was close enough to the fire to dry without catching. Brian took off his gloves. David pulled off his gloves too and held Brian's hands in his. Brian's fingers tingled and then warmed. He put his feet as close to the fire as he dared, to warm them. Soon he was feeling better, and they settled back against the pine boughs. There was nothing else they could do except do their best to stay warm and hope like hell they were found soon. Having David hold him was nice. They were taking care of each other. It had been quite a while since someone other than himself had looked out for him.

"They have to be looking for us. Haven wouldn't wait until the storm is over, would he?"

David shook his head. "No. I suspect he's rounding people up and trying to figure out the best way."

Brian stilled and listened. "Do you hear that?"

David shook his head, but then the sound got more pronounced. It was an engine of some kind. "I hear it now."

"Are there snowmobiles at the ranch?"

"Haven doesn't have any, but Dakota might," David said. "Either that or they called in some favors from some friends." Brian put more wood on the fire to build it up and added some of the green pine branches. That sent billowing smoke up into the wind. He hoped the smoke would signal that they were in the area. They had holed up at the bottom of a slight indentation, so they wouldn't be readily seen.

The engine got louder and louder still. Brian knew someone was very nearby. He added more branches, sending up thicker smoke as the sound of the engine died away. They had to know Brian and David were there. He continued signaling.

"David, Brian, is that you?" Brian looked up as Gus appeared in his line of sight. "Thank goodness I found you."

"David sprained his ankle," Brian said.

Gus nodded and pulled out a phone. He made a call and must have gotten through because he explained where he was and said he'd found both of them. Soon another engine could be heard on the wind. Gus stepped back and disappeared from sight. Brian wondered where Gus had gone, but didn't stick his head up to see what was happening. They had been found and that was what mattered.

"Are you going to be okay to get out of here?" Brian asked, turning to David. "It's going to be difficult."

"I'll make it somehow," David whispered and then went quiet, turning away to stare up at the bare branches above them. Brian added some more wood to the fire, building it up in case the others needed to warm themselves before the trip back. The fire was now putting out plenty of heat. Brian settled back in the shelter and soaked up the warmth. They were going to need it. The wind was fierce and seemed to be getting stronger. Brian pulled David to him.

"They'll be back in a few minutes," Brian said reassuringly. David nodded, but didn't say anything.

"Okay," Gus said as he stood over them, peering down into their shelter. "Gordon is here too. We'll get David out first." He held out his hands and smiled. "That fire feels good, but I think we need to get both of you back to the ranch as quickly as possible."

Brian stood up and shivered against the wind. He helped David to his feet and supported him as he got to the edge of the shelter. Gus practically lifted him out and half carried him across the snow to where Gordon waited on the other snowmobile. Between them, they got David on and then Gordon took off, almost instantly disappearing over the edge of the rise. All Brian could hear was the retreating sound of the engine. "Okay, you're next," Gus said, and Brian climbed out and took a few steps away from the shelter. He couldn't help looking back at the bedding of pine branches that lined the bottom and side. "We should put the fire out," Gus said, and Brian nodded before kicking in the snow wall they'd built. Smoke billowed up and the hiss of dying flame competed momentarily with the wind. Brian kicked some more snow on the dying fire, covering it. Then he turned and followed Gus to the snowmobile.

Gus got on, and Brian climbed behind him, holding him around the waist. He moved as close as he could, the wind and snow already beginning to make their presence known.

"Ready?" Gus asked.

Brian told him yes, and they began to move. The snow passed quickly beneath them. He simply held tight and used Gus's large body as a windbreak. He didn't look around and kept his face covered as best he could. They bounced a little as Gus sped up and they flew over the powder. Brian didn't look until they began to slow and he realized they were approaching the road. Gus turned and they sped alongside the covered pavement before eventually turning into the ranch drive. Gus pulled right up to the front of the house and stopped.

"Thanks," Brian said as he got off.

"I'm glad we found you," Gus said. "I gotta bring this back. But I'll see you later."

Brian nodded, and Gus took off again. He watched as Gus made it to the street and then turned toward Dakota and Wally's. He climbed the steps to the main house and went inside, standing still after he closed the door and letting the warmth surround him. His face tingled, and Brian took off his gloves and wiggled his fingers. He did the same with his toes in his boots. Once he was sure everything was warming and okay, he looked around.

Haven and Phillip both stared at him. David was laid out on the sofa with one foot on a pillow. From the outerwear lying on the floor, it looked like they'd gotten David undressed and settled under blankets. Brian took off his boots and coat and simply let the heat soak in. "Are you hurt?" Phillip asked, getting up from where he'd been sitting on the edge of the sofa next to David.

"No, just cold. I'll be fine," Brian said and stepped toward David, who lay with his eyes closed. "Is he okay?"

"We don't know. He's really cold and the ankle isn't good. Dakota said he would be over as soon as he could." Brian took Phillip's place on the edge of the sofa. He knew his hands were still cold, so he didn't touch David, but he wondered what was wrong with him. "Are you awake?"

"Yes," David whispered. "I'm just tired and starting to warm up again."

Brian moved closer, and David brought his arms from under the blanket and pulled Brian closer. He held David in return, helping to take the chill off him. Neither of them moved. Brian was warming quickly, but it was obvious that David was still very cold. Occasionally, he'd shiver and shake in Brian's arms. Every time it happened, he turned to look at Phillip, wondering what was wrong.

Brian didn't move until he heard the door open and close. Dakota took off his things, and Brian moved away to give him room.

"Tell me what happened," Dakota said.

"We'd found some of the stragglers and sent them on their way back when something under the snow gave way. David told me he'd twisted his ankle really bad and was having trouble walking, so we built a snow shelter and I got a fire started. He said I should go back for help, but I didn't want to leave him. I gathered wood, and we kept a small fire burning until Gus and Gordon found us and brought us back."

"Are you okay?" Dakota asked him, and Brian nodded. "Fingers and toes are fine. We kept each other warm, were out of the wind, and had the fire going. The coldest part was the ride back. At least for me."

"Okay." Dakota began looking David over. David hissed when Dakota moved the blanket to see his ankle, which was already turning purple. "You're running a fever, which isn't surprising. It's part of your body's reaction to the sprain as well as being cold. It's trying to make up for the loss of heat. Normally I'd say to ice the ankle, but I think we need to get you warmed through first. Then, in a few hours, start icing the ankle. Ten minutes on, ten minutes off. I'm going to brace the ankle, which will help it feel better, and it won't hurt as much whenever you try to move it."

David nodded and tensed when Dakota ran his hands along his foot. "I can feel you," David said.

"That's good."

"You're warm," David said. "The last thing I need right now is a doctor with cold hands."

Dakota chuckled softly. David grimaced when Dakota put the brace on his foot and then sighed once it was over. Dakota covered his foot up again and gave David some ibuprofen for the pain. Then he stood up and got ready to leave. "Start icing it once you're good and warmed up. You'll probably have to stay off it for a week or so. It's a bad sprain and it's going to hurt for quite a while. But you were lucky, both of you." Dakota got into his gear and headed for the door. "Let me know if it isn't better tomorrow, and stay off it as much as possible."

"Are you going in to the hospital?" Phillip asked Dakota as Brian settled on the edge of the sofa cushions next to David.

"Yes. They're swamped right now. Apparently, there have been a lot of accidents. People hadn't had a chance to dig out from the last storm before this one came on us, so they're taking chances they probably wouldn't otherwise." Dakota left and pulled the door closed after him.

"Are you feeling better?" Brian whispered to David. He seemed warmer and more comfortable.

"Yeah. I'm rather comfortable. The foot throbs, but it's better now that I have the brace."

"I have lunch started, and it'll be ready in a few minutes," Phillip said and left the room.

"Did the cattle get back?" David asked, turning to Haven.

"We believe we found most of them. The ones you got moving came back, and we got them in with the rest." Haven rested his hand on David's shoulder. "Don't worry about that. Just rest and stay still under the blanket." Haven shook his head. "Between the two of you, I think you've had all the brushes with cold any of us can take this year." Haven walked toward the kitchen and began putting on his gear. "I'm heading back out," he called through the house and went outside. Snow or rain, winter or summer, there was always work to be done on a ranch.

Brian thought about asking if Haven needed help, but David reached for him, so Brian held him. He didn't want to move. They were warm, and David seemed to need him right now. It felt nice to be needed, but he wasn't sure if this was David's signal for something more or just the fact that they'd been through something traumatic and potentially dangerous together. Brian had found that when it came to matters of the heart, he got more confused the more he thought about it. His luck so far had been crap, and he expected that luck to continue. "Can I get you anything?" Brian asked him.

David had to be hungry. Now that he was warm and safe, Brian's own appetite was kicking in. Phillip came in a few minutes later with two plates piled with sandwiches. Brian shifted, and David gingerly sat up. They took the plates, and Phillip hurried away, then returned with two huge, steaming mugs of coffee. "It's a little old, but it's hot and that should really help." Phillip set the mugs on the table and left the room again.

"You saved my life," David said after taking a single bite of his sandwich. "How did you know all that stuff? I was a Boy Scout too, and I wouldn't have known what to do."

Brian set his plate on the coffee table. "Things around my house were anything but normal. I was a Boy Scout, but my dad was a survivalist. He had a stash of food and things in the house. Kept it in one of the closets. He also had an arsenal of guns and ammo. So growing up we had to learn all kinds of stuff like that. We didn't go on camping trips—we went on forages where we either hunted and found food or starved. God, I hated those, my dad barking orders and teaching us how to hunt and fish. He also taught me how to shoot until I was accurate enough to take out a man at a hundred yards. As a kid, he made my first fire-starting kit for me, like the one I used today. He used to ask me where it was, like a pop quiz, and I had to produce it. It got so I always have one. There's even one in the car, but it didn't do me any good the other day."

"Geez, that sounds brutal."

"It's just the way he was. Dad believed, like a lot of people out here, that the government was going to get too big and collapse. Personally, I think he was full of it, but being prepared out here isn't a bad thing, though it's possible to take stuff too far. As I look back on it, things weren't too bad. I mean, he taught me a lot, and we got through the stuff today because of what he taught me. It wasn't fun at the time, but who knew...." He shrugged.

"Well, it came in handy. We might have made it through even if we hadn't have been able to build the fire, but without the shelter and the other things, we could have been in real trouble."

"Probably, but you would have figured things out on your own. At least the shelter part."

"Maybe. But I wouldn't have been able to do much with a sprained ankle other than sit somewhere and shiver until I was found. You helped keep us both warm and reasonably comfortable." David shifted closer, and Brian smiled. "Thank you." David kissed him gently on the cheek, and Brian turned toward him. David leaned close again and kissed his lips.

Brian pressed closer, deepening the kiss and slipping his fingers through David's hair. "You're welcome," he whispered and pulled David closer. They'd gotten so close over the past few hours. They'd kissed before, but this time there was no storm raging around them and no danger. It was simply the two of them sitting on the sofa. He knew they couldn't do very much with Phillip in the next room, but Brian could most certainly signal his interest, and he was sure going to do that in no unmistakable terms. He deepened their kiss, lightly sucking on David's tongue. They broke apart at the sound of a bang from the kitchen. David smiled, and Brian began to chuckle. "Do you think that was on purpose?"

David nodded and reached for his plate. "We need to be good," he whispered. "At least for now."

Brian started eating again too. He was ravenous and quickly finished the sandwich and the coffee. David did the same, and Brian took the plates to the kitchen, where Phillip had more of both ready.

"I have some work to do in the office this afternoon. Holler if either of you needs anything," Phillip said.

"I was going to go out to the barn to help with the horses," Brian said, but Phillip shook his head.

"Haven left strict instructions that neither of you was to be outside today. You both need to be warm and settled for a while. You can go over to the bunkhouse if you really feel the need, but that's about the limit for now. So go ahead and turn on the television if you want and spend some time with daytime TV. It will rot your brain, though." Phillip grinned. "I hate that stuff."

"Okay," Brian said.

"When I first got here I used to do my work in front of the television. Haven was out doing his thing, and I was alone in the house. The television was company, or so I thought. It turned out it was just noise. If you're lucky, you'll find an old movie you can sleep through." Phillip picked up a plate and mug and headed down the hallway. Brian took David's food to him before returning for his own. He settled in one of the chairs to give David room, turned on the television, and proceeded to find nothing at all worth watching. They ended up settling on some battle of the chefs show.

"Does it seem strange to be eating lunch meat sandwiches while they're making pâté de foie gras three ways?" David quipped, and they both made a face. There was no way Brian was eating frou-frou food like that. Yuck. They both laughed and finished their lunch. Once the plates were empty, Brian took them to the kitchen, washed them up, and set them in the drainer to dry. By the time he returned, David's eyes were closed and he was sound asleep, snoring softly. Brian settled in his chair and alternated between watching television and watching David sleep.

"What has you so deep in thought?" Phillip whispered after a while. Brian had lost track of time and hadn't even heard him come into the room. Brian shrugged, and Phillip made a small humphing sound. Brian turned to glance at Phillip and saw him rolling his eyes. "If you don't want to talk, that's cool."

"It's nothing, really," Brian said.

"Okay." Phillip turned and went into the kitchen. Brian heard the coffeepot slip out of the maker and then back in. Then Phillip went back toward his office, and Brian returned his attention to the television and the trials of the chefs trying to cook while at sea. He got drawn into the show and began rooting for various chefs until one of the guys he liked was asked to pack his knives and go. Then he turned off the television, stood up, and watched the wind blow the snow around the yard. A short time later, Haven came in, covered in snow, and began peeling off his outerwear.

"Is everything okay?" Brian asked.

"It will be. The snow is letting up, but the wind seems intent on blowing everything around. We've tightened things down as much as we can. Hopefully this will move on and blow itself out sometime tonight." He didn't sound convinced. "All we need is a break in the weather for a few days and maybe a little sun and warmth, so we can catch our breaths. Have you seen a forecast?"

"They were saying this should end late today or early tomorrow, and then it looked like things were going to get warmer. But they've said that before and changed their minds, so I guess all we can do is prepare for the worst."

Haven humphed and toed off his boots. "I think the worst is upon us. The herd is stressed beyond anything I've ever seen. We're feeding them, but this cold and wind is going to be pulling away more heat than they can generate. It can't go on like this or we're all going to be in real trouble."

Phillip came into the room and hung up Haven's things, then ushered him away. "Quit with the doom and gloom and stop scaring people. Everything is going to be fine. The herd has plenty to eat because of you and the men. They also have shelter from the wind. Yes, it's cold, but not as bad as it was a few days ago, and it's not going to get as cold tonight as it has the last few nights because it's cloudy. So stop worrying. You got back the head you could, and once this is over you can go back out looking, but there can't be many more left out there." Phillip sounded so reasonable and patient, as though he knew exactly how Haven felt and what to say to help him feel better. The two of them were perfect for each other. Brian could see that. What Haven needed, Phillip seemed to provide, and the reverse also seemed true.

"All right, oh wise one," Haven said snarkily, and Phillip took his hand and led him out of the room and down the hallway. Brian put the television back on, turned the volume up slightly, and concentrated on the show, ignoring any other sounds that might have reached his ears.

David started on the sofa, and Brian patted him gently. "Did you have a good nap? How's your foot?"

"It aches," David said. Brian got up and went to the kitchen. He found a Ziploc bag and filled it with ice. Then he got a dishcloth to wrap around it and brought it to David. He lifted the blanket and carefully set it on David's swollen ankle. David hissed in pain and then settled back on the sofa.

Brian could almost feel the tension ratchet up in David's body. "Just ten minutes and then we'll have to take it off," Brian said and noted the time. David hummed his agreement, and Brian put the blanket back in place before sitting back down.

"Does it look bad?" David asked.

"It's turning purple. You're going to have one heck of a bruise." Brian watched as some of the tension left David's features. He'd sprained his ankle a few times, and he knew it hurt like hell for a few days and then it would begin to heal. The ice would take the swelling down, and in another hour or so he'd give David something else for the pain. "Does it just ache, or is the pain really sharp?"

"It's achy and throbby," David said.

That fit with what Brian remembered. "Okay. You can have something for pain in a little while," he said. "It hasn't been long enough yet, and I don't want to give you too much."

David shifted slightly on the sofa. "Why are you doing this? You could just go back to the bunkhouse and rest. You don't need to sit here and fuss over me."

Brian turned, the leather of the chair crinkling as he moved. "Is that what you want me to do? If I'm being a bother, I'll go so I'm not in your way." Brian leaned forward and began to get up.

"I didn't mean it that way. I just didn't want you to feel like you need to play nursemaid. I know you're always active and probably have things you'd rather be doing besides sitting here with me." The wind chose that moment to howl outside the windows. "Okay, well, maybe you don't."

"No. Haven apparently has told everyone he wants them inside and out of the wind."

"You know there isn't much anyone can do when the weather is like this. The wind makes visibility next to zero and goes right through anything we're wearing. The cattle are bred to be hardy: that's all we raise here because the winters and summers are so harsh."

"Yeah. Hopefully this will be over soon, and it's supposed to warm up." He hoped like hell the forecasters were right. Days like this put everyone on edge. They weren't good for the herd or for the men's morale. He figured if he went over to the bunkhouse, he'd find the guys playing poker and drinking. It was what most men did on ranches when they couldn't get outside and had nothing to do. Not that he hadn't done those things on occasion, but for a person who had secrets to keep, alcohol was not something he wanted to add to the mix.

"That's good," David said.

Brian looked at the clock and got back up. He gently removed the ice pack and set it aside.

"It feels better," David said.

"It will when the ice numbs it. When it warms, the pain will return somewhat. We'll put the ice back on in ten minutes." He sat back down, and they returned their attention to the show. Apparently it was some sort of marathon because the channel was running episode after episode of that chef show. Brian was surprised at how engrossed he got. "Are you warm enough?" he asked.

He shifted and sat on the edge of the sofa, careful of David's foot. He just wanted to be closer to him. It was a strange urge, because even with Rocklin he hadn't felt the need to be close to him, at least not like this. He hadn't been sure he should allow himself to get close to David, not after what had happened at the Flying C, but things seemed different here. Part of him wanted to back away, while the other half told him to race forward and hold on with both hands. He wasn't sure what to do, so he decided to do neither. He wasn't going to back away, but he would take it slowly and see where things led. That he could do, because goodness knows he was tired of being alone, especially after being around other couples who seemed so happy and content.

Brian wondered if he should go back to his chair, but David took his hand and held it. Brian leaned back and settled close to David, holding his hand. He was careful not to put too much weight on his legs, but he was comfortable enough and David seemed happy, so they sat together and watched the cooking show. Every ten minutes, Brian would place the ice on David's ankle or remove it. They sat together for hours, content. The only time Brian moved was to empty and refill the Ziploc as the ice melted. Eventually Phillip and Haven joined them and sat together in one of the huge chairs. There wasn't much to do, so they made the best of the downtime.

After a light dinner, which Brian helped prepare, he and David got dressed in their outdoor gear and prepared to make the trip to the bunkhouse. Phillip had offered the use of the guest room, but in the end they decided it would be best if David was settled in his own room. He'd be there for a few days, and David didn't want to impose on Phillip and Haven. Brian figured it was something about being dependent on others, and while he thought David would be better off in the house, he didn't argue. It was David's decision.

They thanked Haven and Phillip and said good night before stepping out into the wind-driven snow. The bunkhouse wasn't too far away, and Brian helped David slowly traverse the distance. He was still relieved when they stepped inside and closed the door behind them. The living area was filled with the other guys, talking, drinking, and yes, playing cards, the way Brian had thought they would. A few were watching football on television, and Brian had to try to remember what day it was. "Who's winning?" he asked and got growls in return. Obviously not the team they had been hoping for.

"Hey, guys, get up," Gus said, scooting the three hands who had crowded together on the old sofa to their feet. "Pull up some chairs—David needs to put that foot up."

"It's all right, thanks," David said. "I'm going to just go to my room. I don't want to disturb everyone." He hobbled down the hallway and into his room, then closed the door behind him.

"You've sure had the worst luck this past week or so. First in the car and then outdoors. Who'd you piss off, anyway?" Gus asked with a smile. Brian chuckled as best he could, but he was starting to wonder if he'd done something, all right. Either someone had it in for him in a cosmic sort of way, or he'd been lucky in dodging a bullet twice in so short a time. He really wasn't sure which, and he sure as hell hoped there wouldn't be a third chance for him to try to figure it out.

"I wish I knew," Brian said and sat down in one of the vacated spots on the sofa.

He spent the next few hours watching nothing much on television. The football game was a total blowout. The team they were rooting for might as well have stayed home. Once he'd had enough, he said good night. He went to his room, closed the door, and got ready for bed.

Brian could hear the guys still playing cards and talking, although the conversation got quieter and quieter as doors opened and closed. Soon the house was silent and the light showing under his door went out. Brian lay on his back, staring up at the ceiling with his hands beneath his head. He'd spent the whole day with David, and it was clear to Brian that David was interested in him. He certainly was interested in David, but he couldn't help wondering if it had simply been all the excitement of being stranded together in the storm. After a while of rolling all this around in his head, he turned onto his side with a snort of derision. Somehow in the past couple of weeks he'd changed from a gay man to a teenage girl, wondering about his feelings and David's feelings. All that touchy-feely stuff was so un-cowboy-like. David liked him, and he liked David. So why analyze the hell out of it? He wanted to go for it, so he should just jump in headlong and see what happened. Sure, it hadn't worked out so well in the past, but this dancing around each other was giving him a damned headache, not to mention a world-class case of blue balls.

He heard movement outside his room and waited for them to pass. But his door opened, and Brian saw David standing in the doorway. Brian jumped out of bed and hurried over to him. "What's wrong? Do you need me to get someone?"

David hobbled inside and closed the door. "My foot is fine, or at least as good as it's going to get right now." David took another step and stumbled. Brian steadied him and guided him toward the bed.

"You need to lie down," Brian said, and he got David settled. "You should have stayed where you were." Brian kept the scolding tone to a minimum. He was happy David was here, but a little confused as well. "Get under the covers so you don't get too cold. Do you need ice for your ankle?"

"Yeah. I also took something for pain and I think it's making me a little loopy."

"What did you take?" Brian asked. He hadn't been aware of Dakota giving David anything for pain.

"One of the pills they gave Hugh last year when he threw his back out. He said to take two, but I only took one. They're really good stuff."

"You shouldn't take other people's prescriptions. What if you were allergic or something?" Brian said and pulled on a pair of sweatpants before leaving the room. He got some ice together and a glass of water before tiptoeing back to his room. He closed the door and carefully placed the ice on David's ankle. David groaned softly, and Brian handed him the glass of water. He drank it all and sighed.

Brian sat on the edge of the bed and waited for ten minutes before removing the ice and setting the bundle aside. He reached over and turned out the light before shucking his sweats and climbing under the covers. "Are you sure you wouldn't be more comfortable in your own bed?" Brian asked. All he got for an answer was David shifting slightly and then throwing an arm around him. "David," Brian whispered into the darkness.

"Yeah."

"Are you really okay with this?" Brian asked. "Your ankle…"

There was no answer. Then David slowly rolled onto his side and pulled Brian right to him. "I have no idea what that other asshole did to you, but…." The words ended when David pulled him into a deep kiss that made Brian's toes and fingers tingle in the best way possible. Brian clung to him, feeling at first like he was sinking down a familiar hole. David shifted slightly, pressing him back onto the mattress. David continued kissing, and Brian arched his back when David splayed his hand over his chest and then used two magic fingers to lightly pluck at one of his nipples.

He knew he had to keep quiet, but Brian desperately wanted to groan and shout. Instead, he held David tighter and swallowed the moans that threatened from David's lips. His entire body shook with nervous excitement as David ran his hands down his sides and continued lower, taking his boxers along with them. Brian sighed slightly when his cock came free of the fabric. He thrust his hips upward, lifting them both off the bed.

The room was dark and Brian wished he could see David, but instead he had to make do with what his hands told him. He stroked down David's lean, strong back, built with years of hard work, to his lower back and then up over the curve where his butt began. He encountered the band of David's boxers and slipped his hands beneath and over his firm, smooth, perfect cowboy ass. Brian grabbed and held on, pressing their hips together. He pushed David's boxer shorts down, and they both moaned softly when their cocks touched for the very first time. Damn, that was exactly what he wanted, and Brian pulled the fabric lower. He needed to get them off, but unless they parted, that wasn't going to happen, and Brian had no intention of breaking the contact between them, not now.

It took a few seconds, but Brian was able to work both pairs of underwear off David's legs and around the bandage on his foot without hurting him. Once he did, he spread his legs and wound them carefully around David. Damn and hell, the man felt good, all muscles and heat. Everywhere Brian touched he felt strong curves: shoulders and arms that had spent years hauling hay, back and chest from muscling fence posts and lifting everything known to man. Even though he couldn't actually see him, Brian's mind filled in the details of what he'd always imagined had been under David's jeans and flannel shirts.

"Do you have anything?" David whispered.

Brian stopped to think, then remembered there might be some supplies in the bottom of his old pack. "Yeah, I think," he answered. David rolled onto the mattress, and Brian jumped off the bed, saying a prayer of thanks to the gods that the bed was silent. If the damn thing had squeaked, they would have been screwed, and not in a good way. He found his pack by the dresser and fumbled around in it. There was a single condom and a mostly empty small bottle of slick, but it would do. Brian returned to the bed with a little too much energy, and it bounced when he jumped back on. He heard David chuckle warmly, and then Brian was struck by David's warmth once again. Somehow he managed to get the supplies on the nightstand as David licked a trail down his chest and belly. "David," Brian whispered. "Oh God, yes." The words were just above a whisper, almost a prayer. He felt David's fingers tighten around him, stroking slowly. He quivered and groaned when the movement stopped, but then he was sucked into the wettest heat he had ever imagined. The sensation was nearly overwhelming, and fuck if he didn't wish he could see David's lips around his cock. "Yeah," he whispered, adding to his erotic murmurs. He thrust his hips slightly, and David took him deeper and harder, nearly all the way.

Brian wasn't sure he was going to live through this, it was so good. When David stopped, he wanted to scream in frustration. But David slowly climbed back up and kissed him hard.

"I want you so bad," David whispered. He slipped a hand between Brian's legs, lightly teasing his opening with a single finger. Brian shivered with excitement and made sure David felt it. David's finger slipped away, and Brian held his breath. It was so dark he couldn't see what was happening, but soon the finger returned, and this time it was wet. David made tiny circles around his opening before sliding the tip of his finger inside him. Brian vibrated with unbridled excitement and pulled David closer, deepening the kiss as David pressed deeper inside him.

"Have you done this before?" David asked.

"Yeah, I'm not some blushing virgin," Brian answered.

David stopped. "I think you are, in a way." He made small circles inside him, and Brian trembled with the desire to scream to the rafters, it felt so good.

"Oh, yeah?" Brian challenged.

"Yup," David whispered into his ear before sucking on it. "But I think I'm going to show you rather than tell you." David pushed his finger deeper and curled it slightly. Brian gasped, and David kissed away the sound as desire and pleasure bloomed from deep inside him.

"Holy hell," Brian whispered and wondered what else David had to show him. David did it again, and soon Brian was quivering, his cock bouncing against his belly in throbs of wanton passion. He felt David shift on the bed and helped him retrieve the things from the nightstand.

Slowly David's finger retreated, and Brian stifled a groan. He heard a package open and waited, trying to imagine what David looked like as he rolled the condom down his cock. He wanted to see and was tempted to turn on the light, but it would be too bright and he didn't want to kill the mood. There was something special, intimate, about being together in the dark. He could imagine that it was just the two of them and that nothing else mattered.

David circled his opening with his finger once again, and this time it was slick. It slipped inside and was quickly followed by another. The stretch felt amazing, and Brian hissed softly with need. After a few seconds, David pulled his fingers away, and Brian's muscles went wild at the emptiness.

David shifted his weight, pressing against him as Brian felt David's cock push into him. Brian relaxed and stroked down David's back, grabbing his ass and urging him forward. He wanted this badly, and as David entered his body, he buried his face in his shoulder to keep from crying out as a flash of pain morphed into a sunrise of unbelievable ecstasy. He gasped for air, mouth hanging open. When he could breathe, David's scent entered him just as surely as David's cock slowly pressed deeper and deeper, stretching and filling him. David stopped, and Brian pulled him forward. The last thing he wanted was for this to stop for any reason.

Brian was over the moon, and when he felt David's hips tight to his, he held still and concentrated on drawing oxygen into his lungs. Then, after a few moments, David began to move. Brian closed his eyes and gave himself over to the sensation. He bit his lower lip to keep from crying out when David retreated and from shouting every sexy obscenity he could think of when David's thick cock slid back into him.

"Damn, you feel amazing around me," David whispered. "Like you were made for me and me alone."

Brian hummed his agreement and did his best not to read too much into those words. He wanted to let his heart soar at the simple declaration, but he held it in check and moved back and forth with David, meeting long, slow thrusts that dragged David's cock perfectly over that spot inside him, fucking again and again. His mind took off and soon he was telling David everything he wanted him to do.

"I'll do all that and more," David whispered, and Brian realized that what he'd thought he'd been saying in his mind he'd been muttering out loud for David to hear.

"You will?" Brian asked.

"Fuck yeah. I'll take you to heaven and back if you let me," David whispered in his ear and picked up speed. Soon Brian forgot about everything except David and the way he was making his body sing. No one had ever done that before, and suddenly Brian knew what he'd been missing.

"I think I'm already there," Brian whispered. He reached between them and grabbed his cock, stroking himself while David drove him upward on a rocket trajectory. He couldn't last much longer. David was breathing deeply, and soon Brian's breathing fell in time with his, just like the rest of his body seemed to. "Damn it, I'm so close." He wanted this to last, but he was so keyed up he knew he'd tumble over the edge at any second. David picked up his pace, and Brian did as well. Soon he opened his eyes, concentrating on anything other than coming, but it was too much and he shot, spilling his ecstasy onto his belly while David throbbed deep inside him. Then they stilled, and there was only the sound of their breathing in the small room.

Brian didn't move an inch. He held David still as he floated on clouds of warmth. Slowly, David began to shift gingerly. Their bodies separated, and David rolled onto his back next to him. Brian turned on his side and moved closer, lightly stroking David's smooth chest. He wanted to ask if David's ankle was okay, but it seemed like a mood killer, so he rested his head on David's shoulder and lay still.

"Are you sore?" David whispered.

"No. Are you?" Brian asked and got up. He found a towel and used it to clean them both up, then pulled on his sweats and quietly left the room. He got some more water and hurried back. David might need another painkiller later. When he returned, he saw David staring at him in the dim light from the hallway. Brian closed the door, gave David some more water, and then slipped off his sweats and climbed into bed. The bunkhouse was quiet, and Brian let David get comfortable before rolling on his side and moving closer. "Is your ankle okay?"

"Yes," David whispered and tugged him closer.

"You didn't hurt it during…?"

"No. I was careful and kept pressure off it as much as I could, but I had more important things on my mind." David's smile was wickedly delightful, but Brian saw pain in his eyes and wasn't so sure David was being completely honest. But he let it go… for now.

"It's been a long time since I slept with anyone. I hope I don't kick or something."

David hummed and simply held him closer. Brian closed his eyes and drifted happily toward sleep. He didn't want to think about the possibilities of what could happen in the morning. His experience with that sort of thing was not exactly stellar. In fact, he'd never spent the night with a lover before. Things had always been rather rushed and furtive. As he listened to David's soft breathing, he hoped like hell nothing happened to mess this up.

Chapter Four

DAVID WOKE next to Brian. At first he tried to remember where he was and why he was there. He'd had weird dreams and remembered taking some pain medication that must have made him a little loopy. The first thing he remembered clearly was spending the night with Brian. His ankle ached like hell and he needed something for the pain. But as he slowly rolled onto his side, he realized he needed something else as well. Brian was still sound asleep, and David let a hand travel under the covers and then glide over Brian's back. He rubbed slowly, and Brian rolled onto his belly and mumbled something he couldn't understand. It was still early and David listened. The wind seemed to have died away, which meant everyone would be up soon. There would be a lot of work to get done, and if the sun came out and warmed things up, that would mean additional work cleaning up from the storms.

"Brian," David said softly, smiling when Brian rolled over and cracked his eyes open.

"Hey," Brian said with a grin. "I guess I didn't dream last night after all."

"Nope," David said and pushed back the covers. "I don't know how you feel about the guys knowing what happened last night, but they're going to figure it out as soon as they see me coming out of your room."

Brian shrugged. A few days earlier he would have worried, but not now. "Is it still storming?" he asked with a yawn.

"I don't think so," David answered. "I haven't heard the wind, so I bet it's going to be a busy day."

"Yeah. Digging out again." Brian sat up, the covers pooling around his waist.

David propped his head on his hand on one hand and with his other slowly stroked along Brian's chest. The muscles weren't huge and defined like pictures of guys he'd seen in skin mags. This was what he expected from a cowboy—lean muscles from hard work and the scars from life. David moved closer, wanting to tug Brian down into a kiss and begin an encore of last night. But footsteps in the hall followed by the voices of the men as they got up and began moving around put an end to that idea. Some of the guys were gay, but most were straight, and while they were supportive, he figured there was no need to put on a show.

"I better get up," Brian said. "They aren't going to expect to see you anyway, so stay here and relax. I'll bring you some ice and something for pain." Brian smiled at him and then leaned close. They shared a quick kiss, and then Brian got out of bed. David watched Brian's bare cowboy butt as he wandered around the room, and he stifled a groan as Brian stepped into his underwear and an old pair of jeans. Then he took them off again and David wondered if he was being treated to a show.

"Is that for me?" David asked with a smile.

Brian turned around and flashed him a smile. "I remembered that I was going to need something warmer," he said. He pulled on a pair of boxer briefs and then long underwear. "Sexy, isn't it?" he quipped and then laughed outright.

The sound was like music, warm and deep, wrapping around him. David didn't remember feeling like that with Mario. As soon as the thought entered his mind, he pushed it away fast. He didn't want to think about or be reminded of Mario right now. But that was unfinished business. It had been six months since he'd returned, and almost two years since he'd left. It was time to put it behind him. That is, if he wanted a chance to be with Brian.

"It's perfect," he said, returning Brian's smile. "Now go on and get dressed before half the men come in here to figure out if there's something wrong." David watched Brian finish getting dressed. He figured he'd return to his own room once everyone had left.

It didn't take Brian long, and once he was dressed, he leaned over the bed. "Please stay off your foot and let it heal. I suspect our mother hen will be over to make sure you have lunch, but if I can, I'll come see if you need anything."

David wanted to tell Brian he didn't need to worry, but it felt nice to have someone fuss over him and care what happened to him again. He'd screwed it up the last time and he didn't want to do that again. So he would take what Brian wanted to give and be grateful for it. "I'll see you later." Brian kissed him and then left the room.

"Morning, Brian," he heard through the cracked-open door. It must not have closed completely. "There's coffee if you want some." It had to be Gus. No one else was that damned chipper in the morning. "I'll take some to David."

"I can do it if you like," Brian said, and David waited. After a bit, Brian came into the room, and as soon as he pushed open the door, a series of catcalls and whistles filled the house. Brian turned beet red. "I should have gone to your room."

David nodded. "They know now," he observed, and Brian brought him the coffee before leaving the room.

"What are you, two-year-olds?" Brian said as soon as he stepped outside the room.

There was unmistakable tension in his voice. The other men laughed and continued teasing, which David figured was a good thing. Whatever had happened at Brian's other ranch, it wouldn't happen here. The bosses wouldn't stand for it, and the men were all really tolerant.

"So I take it you want to hear all about it," Brian said loudly, to a chorus of "Too much information."

"Okay, then." The guys laughed. Conversation continued to drift into the room. David sipped his coffee and then set the cup on the nightstand. He rolled over and closed his eyes, Brian's scent still bright and rich on the bedding.

The voices from the other room faded as the men left for the day, and once all was quiet, he drifted back to sleep and woke a few hours later. His ankle throbbed and ached, so David got up and found some pain pills. He took them and hobbled to his room to dress. There was very little he could do, but he was determined not to sit around all day, so once he was done, he looked out the window at the sun shining brightly off the fresh blanket of snow. It was nearly blinding. He couldn't see much other than the rangeland that stretched unbroken as far as he could see.

A soft knock from behind him made him jump slightly. "I brought you some breakfast." It was Phillip, and David turned around and slowly hobbled toward him. "Come on out to the living room."

"Thank you," David said and followed Phillip out of his room and down the hall to the living area.

"I heard a rumor that you had a particularly good night last night." Phillip brought him a plate from the kitchen, and David settled on the sofa and put his leg up. It instantly felt better. "You know this place is like gossip central. Forget about women. Put twelve guys in close proximity, add in a few who are gay, and you have the gossipiest place on earth." Phillip sat in the nearest chair. "God, I need to get rid of this furniture and see about some new pieces. This stuff is terrible." He scooched around in the chair until he got comfortable.

David began to eat and waited for Phillip to say what was on his mind.

"You seem unusually solemn for someone who had such a good night. What gives?" Phillip asked.

"Nothing at all," David answered.

Phillip rolled his eyes. "You guys are all just like Haven. You'd rather wrestle a steer to the ground than talk about what you're feeling. Mind you, it isn't a requirement." Yet Phillip settled in the chair and didn't seem like he was in any hurry to leave. David concentrated on the food in front of him rather than on Phillip. He so did not want to talk about this.

"Fine," he said once he was done and couldn't ignore him any longer. "It's…."

Phillip nodded, but that was the only movement he made. "You know this is your home," Phillip said after a while. "When you first came back, we expected this to be temporary, but you're a good worker and good for the ranch."

"Thanks," David said.

"But I expected you and Mario would have made your peace by now." Phillip stood up. "Maybe that's what's bothering you." Phillip took the plate, walked toward the kitchen area, and set it on the counter. "I'll see you later. Maybe if you're feeling up to it, you can come to the house for lunch." He put on his coat, grabbed the plate, and headed for the door.

"Thanks, Phillip. I really appreciate it," David called. Phillip waved and hurried out into the cold sunshine. He closed the door behind him, and David stared at the four walls, wondering what in the hell he was going to do. He desperately hated just sitting around with nothing to do. He turned on the television and ended up watching nothing. Hell, he was relieved when a few hours later the chef competition show he'd watched the day before with Brian came on. Eventually, he hobbled to the refrigerator and got some ice for his ankle before sitting back down and willing the time to go faster. Of course it didn't.

AT ABOUT lunchtime, he decided he'd sat around long enough, so he put on his gear and made his way as carefully as he could across the yard to the main house. He saw Gus heading into the barn and raised his hand in greeting, but continued on his way. He'd hoped to see Brian, but he didn't seem to be anywhere around.

David knocked, and Phillip opened the door and ushered him inside. He carefully went in and took off his gear. Phillip motioned for him to head to the table, where Mario and Gordon were already seated. David should have known something was up, and he glared at Phillip, who pointedly ignored him. David sat down, and Phillip brought salad and soup to the table.

"Is this one of your schemes?" Mario asked Phillip.

"Hey," Gordon said lightly and patted Mario's hand.

Mario drew it back fast and glared at the former Marine. "You knew about this?" he asked.

"I think it's their way of saying that we need to come to some sort of closure," David said, to get the others off the hook. "You've moved on and I'm happy for you. Gordon is a good man, and he obviously makes you happy." Hell, it hurt sometimes to see how happy the two of them were together. But he'd gotten over it.

"You still left," Mario said, ignoring the bowl of soup Phillip set in front of him.

"I know that," David snapped, ignoring the other people in the room. "But you know things hadn't been good between us, so I left. Would you have wanted me to stay? Knowing how things turned out for you, would you still have wanted me to stay?" David looked at Gordon and saw Mario do the same thing. "It worked out for the best for you, and like I said, you deserve to be happy. I made a mistake." David picked up his spoon—he needed something to do with his hands.

David glanced at Phillip and thought about just getting up from the table. This was a bad idea on so many levels. Mario was hardheaded and hot-blooded; he always had been. Yes, David had left, and he'd hurt him, but Mario had moved on with Gordon and they were happy, as far as David could tell.

"You didn't even try to work things out," Mario said. "You just upped and left when things got tough. Is that what you're going to do with Brian?"

David jumped to his feet, knocking the table and sloshing soup out of the bowls, but he didn't give a damn. "Leave him out of this. I apologized and have tried to stay out of your way so you and Gordon could build a relationship because I thought that's what you wanted. You made it very clear that things were over between us months ago. So the only reason I can come up with for why you're being such a shit is because they aren't as over as you want to think they are." David glared at Mario, and then sat back down before shifting his gaze to Gordon, who looked as though he'd been shot through with an arrow.

"Is that true?" Gordon asked.

"No. It's not true," Mario said. "I am over him."

"Then I suggest you let whatever you have stuck in your craw go. Because it isn't good for you, me, or the ranch." Gordon turned toward Phillip. "I have some work to get done." He stood and left the room, heavy footsteps leaving no doubt as to the big man's hurt.

"Fuck," David said softly as he watched Gordon go. "Happy now?" he spat at Mario, who looked shocked and beaten.

"I didn't... I wasn't the one who...."

"The hell you weren't," David began, working up a bigger head of steam. "Everything was always my fault. Whenever anything went wrong, it was my fault. If you forgot to do the dishes, it was somehow my fault for not reminding you. Well, that isn't going to work anymore. I'm not there to blame, and you can try to pin the demise of our relationship totally on me if it makes you feel better, but you had just as much a hand in it as I did." David tried to lighten his tone. "I think it's time we forgave each other so we can both move on."

Mario wasn't buying it—David could tell by the way his nostrils flared with each breath. His fire had been part of what had attracted David in the first place. But eventually the stubbornness had worked on him. "Yeah... well...."

"Gordon loves you. There's no doubt about that, and you're happy with him. I have no intention of trying to come between the two of you. So let it go and allow yourself to be happy. You deserve it. Hell, we all deserve it."

Mario said nothing, but alternated between looking down at his plate and toward the door. Eventually he stood up, grabbed his things, and rushed out of the house.

David felt like shit. He'd gone too far and hurt both Mario and Gordon. He dropped back into his seat and spooned some soup into his mouth.

"Jesus," Phillip muttered. "I thought this would be easy."

David nearly choked on his soup. "You have to be kidding. Mario never let anything go in the three years we were together. I know you were with him for a while before you met Haven. Was he that impossible then?"

"No, because we were just having a good time—he wasn't in love with me, and I wasn't in love with him. I thought I was once, but he was with you, and I was lucky enough to meet Haven." Phillip sighed. "Don't worry too much about it. He and Gordon need to talk. Things will work out. Once he realizes what he has and what he's putting in jeopardy, he'll see what's important."

"I hope so. Because Gordon is a really great guy from what I've seen, and he looks at Mario as though he hung the moon. He always has. Even last summer, with those problems with the drug dealers and people who kept trying to set Wally's cats free, he was there for Mario the entire time."

"Yeah," Phillip said, chewing his lower lip. "Go on and eat. I really wasn't expecting all this drama, and I made way too much food."

David did as Phillip said, thinking the entire time that he should have simply kept his mouth shut. Mario would have thawed eventually on his own. But he'd pushed, and now, thanks to David's big mouth, he'd succeeded in pushing Mario into a corner. He finished eating a now rather quiet lunch, then thanked Phillip for trying and went back to the bunkhouse.

Maybe it would be best if he simply didn't get involved with anyone he worked with. Things were bad enough between him and Mario. What if they went the same way between him and Brian? He didn't want that to happen. Hell, he hadn't meant for things to get so messed up between him and Mario. God, sometimes love made things crazy. Well, not love so much as when love ended. David settled on the sofa, elevated his foot, and sat watching television until he heard the other guys outside. Then he got up, hobbled down to his room, and closed the door. He wasn't in the mood to see a lot of people. David stretched out on his bed and closed his eyes. He just needed a chance to think things through.

He listened as the men gathered in the living area. He half expected to hear a recap of what had happened over lunch, but the men simply talked about their day, and he was grateful not to be the topic of conversation.

A soft knock sounded on his door. "David?" The door opened slowly and Brian stepped inside. "Are you okay? Is your ankle hurting?"

"Yeah, I'm okay. The ankle hurts, but not as much as it did yesterday," David said.

"Okay. Then what's wrong?" Brian came closer. "You're hiding in here instead of being out there with the guys, even after having been alone for most of the day."

"Did Phillip send you?" David pressed, staring at Brian as he came closer.

"No, but I guess that means something did happen."

David sighed. "I went to the house for lunch. Mario and Gordon were there. I think it was Phillip's way of trying to get Mario and me to come to some sort of closure. It didn't go well." David shook his head slowly. "He got testy, and I got angry and ended up hurting him and Gordon. It was a mess, and I feel like a huge steaming pile. Gordon's a good guy, and I really like him. Phillip was just trying to help, but he ran up against the stubborn wall that is Mario, with my own bullheadedness thrown in."

Brian sat on the edge of the bed, and David moved his legs so his foot was comfortable. "Okay, so what do you want to do about it?"

"I suppose going over there and shaking Mario until he gets some sense isn't a good idea. But, I mean, he's hanging on to... whatever, from when we broke up, and he doesn't want to let it go. He's basically moved on with Gordon, though, and I want some closure as well. I mean, we work at the same place—it would be good if we could get to a place where we can be friends and colleagues instead of simply tolerating each other when we're in the same room."

"You seemed to be okay at the poker game," Brian observed.

"We are, generally. As long as no one brings up the subject that we used to be together or asks us to actually spend time around each other without 'adult supervision.' He hates me for leaving, and I get that, but I proved that I cared about the ranch and everyone here last summer when I got shot trying to protect this place." Brian gasped, and David realized he hadn't told him about that. "I'll tell you the whole story later. I promise."

"Is that where you got the scar on your shoulder?"

"Yeah. Anyway, I trust Gordon and I know he'll make Mario happy. The man adores Mario. So why can't that be enough for him?"

Brian didn't answer right away. Not that David really expected an answer. "When you left, I suspect you took some part of Mario with you and he hasn't figured out how to get it back yet." David gaped in astonishment. That had to be it. But he wasn't sure what that part might be. "Maybe he isn't as confident as he was before, or as secure in his relationships." Brian sat on the edge of the bed. "Being hurt does strange things, I guess, and it isn't rational."

"No, it isn't," David agreed. "But I'm afraid I made things worse."

"I doubt that." Brian shrugged. "Maybe getting angry is what will finally allow him to let it go? I can tell you this much: it has to come from him. He has to be willing to move on. I figured that he probably would, having Gordon in his life and all. It would be easier if you weren't around. That way he would be free to just hate you."

"Yeah, I suppose he would," David said. "I guess I can talk to Phillip to make sure Mario and Gordon are okay. Other than that, it's up to him." He sighed. "But he's being so stupid."

"Well, maybe. But it doesn't feel stupid to him."

David realized he was right. Whatever Mario had stuck in his stubborn brain was his problem, and no one would get Mario to change his mind unless he wanted to.

"I think the guys are making some dinner."

David was grateful for the change in the subject.

"Are you going to come out and join everyone?" Brian asked.

David slid to the edge of the bed and stood up. He slowly made his way toward the door and followed Brian to the living area. He settled into one of the chairs.

"Are you and Brian an item, or was last night just the two of you knocking boots?" Luke, one of the older hands, asked.

David looked at Brian, not sure how to answer right away. "We're trying to figure that out, I think," he answered. It hadn't felt like just pent-up pressure to him, but he didn't want to speak for Brian. "It's new," he finally said with a smile he couldn't stop.

"Well, of course it's new. He ain't been here but a week or so." Luke sounded exasperated, and David wondered if there was a problem. "Just don't be keeping everyone up at night with your hijinks, 'cause Lord knows the rest of us don't want to hear it." There was more venom in Luke's voice than David would have expected. He looked to the other guys, and they had all turned away, either pretending they hadn't heard or were otherwise occupied.

Brian looked distinctly uncomfortable, lightly rubbing the back of his neck, and David suspected he was trying to figure out a graceful way to leave the room. Granted, David agreed that if he and Brian were together, they owed the other men the respect of being quiet. Hell, they owed each other the same respect; they weren't putting on some kind of show for the bunkhouse.

"You mean the way you keep everyone awake snoring like some demon from hell," Brian retorted, and the other men began to laugh.

"I don't think you got anything to worry about, Luke. They'd have to be awful loud to drown you out," Gus called from the kitchen area. Luke was notorious for snoring loud enough to keep the entire bunkhouse awake. On more than one occasion, David could have sworn the man was in the room with him, and they didn't even have rooms next to each other.

Luke scowled. "This is a bunkhouse, not a cathouse."

"It's not a monastery either," Brian countered rather quickly, and that seemed to take some of the wind out of Luke's sails. David glanced at Brian and figured he was just getting warmed up.

"Well, just keep it quiet," Luke huffed and thankfully said no more.

"I'm heading into town after supper. Does anyone need a lift?" Gus asked. No one spoke up.

"I'll ride with you if you want some company," David volunteered. He was getting more than a little tired of these four walls, and even just a ride into town would be a pleasant change of scenery. David got up and helped the guys get the table ready. He knew he shouldn't spend a lot of time on his feet, but he really needed to move around and do something. Once dinner was ready, they all sat down. Dinners were usually rather raucous affairs with multiple conversations going on at once, and this was no exception. Everyone talked at the same time, laughed, and generally had a good time and got along. Afterward, David helped with cleanup and got ready to leave with Gus. He had hoped that Brian would come along, but he seemed content to relax with the other guys.

"He's prob'ly tired," Gus noted as they went to leave. David shrugged. It wasn't as though they were joined at the hip or anything.

David made his way to the truck and climbed in, stretching out his leg and making sure his foot was comfortable. It wasn't hurting as much, and he figured in a few days he'd be able to walk okay as long as he continued to use the brace and didn't lift too much. Riding would be an issue, but he'd just have to take it easy and let the ankle heal. He figured he should check with Haven about what sort of things he wanted him to do.

"I hate just sitting," David said at one point as they rode. Thankfully, the roads were clear of snow and fairly dry.

"We all do. At least it ain't as bad as when you were shot. You'll be up and around again in no time."

"I know." For a guy whose life had always been filled with activity, being forced to sit was driving him crazy, just like it had that past summer. "Where are we headed?"

"I have to pick up some supplies, and the hardware store is open late, so I figured I could get out a bit and save myself a trip in the morning," Gus explained. "Haven has a list, and I thought I could get a jump on it."

"You were going stir-crazy too," David said.

"Yeah. Sitting inside watching the snow was not my idea of fun," Gus told him.

They pulled into a parking spot in front of the hardware store and got out.

"I have some things I need next door, so I'll meet you back here," David said. He didn't want to make a big deal over going to the drugstore for some supplies he hoped he and Brian would need. It wasn't anyone's business, and he wondered if he could get in and out without much fuss.

Gus had his own list of things to do, so David headed down the sidewalk and into the brightly lit drugstore. Thankfully, there weren't many people shopping, and David was able to get what he needed and take it to the register without encountering anyone he knew. That ended when he saw the checkout lady staring at him.

"Evening, Shirley," David said, instantly wanting to drop through the floor. Shirley Smith knew all and told all. At least that was her reputation. He placed the box on the counter, and she scanned it and told him how much.

"So, everything going okay?" Shirley asked as he handed her the bills and she placed the condoms in a bag. "There hasn't been anything come up missing out at your place, has there?"

That was a leading question if he ever heard one. David wondered what she was up to. "No." He waited for his change and figured it was best not to encourage her and just get out of there.

"Really…?" she said with well-practiced surprise. "If I were you, I'd be sure to keep an extra eye on my stuff." She handed him his change, and David took his bag and headed for the door.

"Thanks, Shirley, you have a great night," he called just before leaving. David walked to the truck and stashed his purchase under the seat before slowly heading into the hardware store. He didn't see Gus right away and wasn't in the mood to wander through the store, so he went up to the front counter.

"Looking for Gus? He's in the back with Uncle Frank," Jeff told him. The kid couldn't have been much more than twenty, and as cute as a button. David always figured the kid had to be beating them off with a stick.

"Thanks," David said and leaned against the counter, lifting his injured foot off the floor. He wished there was a place he could sit down, but the store was crammed from floor to ceiling with merchandise. He swore there wasn't a square inch left anywhere.

"Sprain your ankle?" Jeff inquired.

"Out in that last blizzard," David said. His foot was really starting to ache, and he realized this trip probably hadn't been a good idea. He hoped Gus would be ready soon so they could head back and he could put his foot up. "I was trying to bring in a few stray head and twisted my ankle on something under the snow."

"That's tough luck," Jeff said as he lounged forward on the counter. The place was really quiet, and David figured Jeff was only there to make sure no one ran off with the store.

"Are you usually open this late?"

"Just a few nights a week. Uncle Frank thought it would increase business if he stayed open until folks were done with work. It doesn't seem to have made much of a difference, but a few people have come in." Jeff straightened up as Gus approached the counter with a handbasket full of stuff. He placed it on the counter and worked with Jeff to arrange to have the bulky portion of the order—fence wire and posts—delivered out to the ranch.

"Haven said to put it all on the ranch account and to send out a bill right away so we can pay you," Gus explained to Jeff, who got to work ringing up everything. "Is there anything new going on?" Gus asked while Jeff worked.

"Not much. Milford is expecting a new crop of horses in the next few months, I understand. I'm hoping my dad will line up one of the colts for me. Trixie is still doing well, but I need to start to train a new horse for roping and such. She's starting to get old, and Milford has the best horses." Jeff continued working and talking. "I heard there's a new hand out at your place. Seems like a strange time of year for a ranch to be hiring." Jeff finished up at the register and prepared the receipt.

David had been half listening to the exchange, but now Jeff had his full attention.

"Well, you never know," Gus said and glanced over at David as if to tell him not to say anything he didn't want all over town.

"Some guys from the Flying C were in a few days ago. They don't usually buy their things from Uncle Frank, but he's been trying to get their business, so they came in between the storms and stocked up." He was obviously proud of his uncle, which he had a right to be. Frank Marshall had built the hardware business up to where it was nearly indispensable to everyone in the area. "They were saying they fired some guy from out there."

"Did they say why?" David asked, trying not to sound too interested.

"I didn't ask and neither did Uncle Frank, but I heard them talking about not wanting any"—Jeff swallowed and paused—"fags. Their word, not mine," he added hastily, "on their ranch. They were talking amongst themselves about how they fixed him good, even if the boss wasn't so keen on it." Jeff began bagging up the purchases, then handed Gus the receipt and had him sign the slip for the billing. Then he gave Gus a copy of the receipt. "Do you need help loading?"

"No, I got it," Gus said and lifted most of the bags off the counter. "We need to get."

"Thanks for coming in," Jeff said with a smile. David took the remaining bags and followed Gus to the truck. They stowed everything and climbed in. Sitting down felt glorious, and so did the heat once Gus started the engine.

"The rumors sure are flying," David commented softly.

"You know how ranch folks talk, especially when they want to make sure folks are on their side," Gus said. "Firing someone this time of year is pretty dang low, if you ask me."

"Yeah, it is, and it sounds like what Brian told me was the truth. He said the men had been sabotaging him so he'd look bad," David commented. "What Jeff said fits that."

Gus backed out of the parking space and put the truck in gear, then slowly headed out of town and into the countryside. "Sounds like it."

David nodded and scratched the back of his head. "Shirley at the drugstore asked me if anything had gone missing."

Gus nodded. "Frank was working in the back, and he hinted at the same sort of thing. Said we should all keep an eye on our things."

"What do you think that's about?" David asked.

"Don't know. But most of the conversation and gossip seems to center around the Flying C and the fact that they let someone go." Gus slowed down and glanced over at him. "Jeff just about said that the men there wanted to get rid of him, so maybe now that he's gone, they're spreading lies, especially now that they know he has a new job and stuff." Gus huffed softly. "I don't rightly understand folks who go around hating other people for no reason. It doesn't make sense to me unless they hate themselves so much that they can't stand to see other folks happy."

"What should we do?" David asked.

"Nothin'," Gus said. "People jaw about stuff all the time. Don't mean anything, and tomorrow they'll have something new to talk about. If they're talking about Brian, then he don't need to know about it. Folks can be dumb sometimes, and most of it's prob'ly blown out of proportion anyhow."

David nodded and went back to watching the inky blackness outside the windows. The headlights from other cars pierced the night, but the black closed in as soon as they passed. David figured Gus was right and nothing good would come from listening to rumors, but he couldn't help wondering if there wasn't something more to this whole story than he'd been told. He huffed out his breath softly. He didn't want to think anything bad about Brian, but the doubt crept in like a snake in the barn, hiding under the straw and waiting to strike.

Chapter Five

BRIAN LOVED Sundays. It was the one day on a ranch when everyone only did what needed to get done and then spent the rest of the day relaxing, sleeping, or in some cases sleeping off Saturday night. He woke with David wound around him in the cool room. Thankfully, there had been a break in the conveyor belt of winter storms. The sun had come out for the past three days and warmed things up enough that some of the snow had melted and the cattle were able to catch their breaths, which made Haven much easier to be around. Though now he was watching the creek at the back of the property, wondering if it was going to flood. There was no making him happy sometimes.

"What are you chuckling about?" David mumbled.

"Nothing," he whispered. "Go back to sleep. I was just thinking how Haven is never happy."

David rolled over. "That's 'cause he's a ranch owner. There are a million things to worry about when it's your ass on the line every day." David tugged Brian closer. "Why are you thinking about him at a time like this? Aren't I enough for you?"

Brian lightly slapped David's arm and closed his eyes again. He'd been handling everything in the barn since David had been laid up, and he was exhausted. Dakota had said that David wasn't to return to work until Monday. He wanted to make sure the ankle had a good chance to heal. David had spent the past few days grousing and hanging around the barn just to avoid sitting in the bunkhouse all day. He'd pushed Dakota's ruling a little, but Brian wouldn't tell as long as David was taking it easy.

They fell back to sleep for a little while and woke to a thud from the living area. Obviously the guys were up and trying to say that they should be getting up as well. The others knew they were using one room and had said nothing more about it as long as they were quiet.

"I was hoping to have a little fun this morning," David whispered before licking one of Brian's nipples.

Brian shuddered and moaned almost silently. "You know they're out there and will give us crap if they hear anything."

"Then maybe we should give them something to listen to," David said with a grin and began to bounce on the bed.

Brian laughed and moved away. "Come on. They've been really good, and they don't have to be, so we should be considerate."

David humphed and started to get up as well. Brian pulled on his underwear and watched as David wandered through the room, his white butt bobbing slightly as he moved. "I think when we get some vacation time, we should get you someplace with some sun," Brian teased.

"Look who's talking," David countered, pointing at Brian's legs.

"Yeah, I know. This time of year is not conducive to anything other than pale and pasty." It took Brian a few seconds to realize what he'd said. He'd actually talked about them taking a vacation together, and David hadn't balked or even blinked at the idea. That was a happy discovery. If he'd have said something like that to Rocklin, the closet case, he would have come unglued and then gone out of his way to cover up and make sure that everyone knew he was interested in girls. "I thought that once I get the chores done, we could go into town. Haven got me some gas for the car, and I need to get into town so I can fill it up. I hear there's a theater in town, and Gus said they were playing one of those movies where they blow everything up."

David chuckled as he continued dressing. He pulled on his jeans and then sat down on the edge of the bed. He put on his socks and then Velcroed on the splint before putting on his shoes. "I could deal with explosions."

That was one thing they'd found they had in common. Brian loved disaster movies and alien invasions, as well as car-chase movies that ended in explosions. And, of course, James Bond, especially the newer ones where Daniel Craig ran around in next to nothing. "Maybe we could have some lunch too."

David turned to him and smiled. "Are you asking me out on a date?"

Brian hadn't thought about it that way, but he smiled in return. "I guess I am." David nodded, and they continued getting dressed. Once they were ready, Brian opened the door and they both stepped out.

Luke was making breakfast. During the week it was usually something filling and fast, but on Sundays he made his famous flapjacks. He was standing at the stove, flipping pancakes and soaking in the praise for his cooking. Gus had told him it was the only thing Luke knew how to make, but Brian didn't care. The pancakes were good, Brian couldn't argue with that. He took a seat at the table and waited for Luke to put a stack on his plate. Luke did the same for David and then went back to the griddle.

They ate the hearty breakfast, and then Brian headed out to take care of the horses. He needed to make sure they had feed and water. He also wanted to put them in their paddocks for a few hours while the temperatures were moderate. It would let them stretch their legs and help keep the barn clean.

He fed and watered the horses, then gave them time to eat before placing them in the paddocks. He decided to do some more spot cleaning of the stalls before sweeping the floors and making sure everything was in shape. After he finished, he brought the horses back inside so they could finish eating. The barn smelled clean and felt warm and rather cozy by the time he was done. The horses were content and had everything they needed, and the dogs lounged in their spot in the corner, jumbled in a pile to help keep warm. It felt like the entire ranch was letting out a sigh of relief after the last stressful couple of weeks. "That's it, guys. Just take it easy today. I'm going to." Brian paused and looked down the aisle. He used to always talk to the horses on the ranch when he was growing up. They had been his companions and friends, along with the dogs. But he hadn't talked to horses in years. At the other ranches he'd worked at, including the Flying C, he'd always been afraid he might say something he shouldn't and the other men would overhear or simply think him strange. So he'd kept quiet.

Brian smiled to himself and took a deep breath. The tension that had been present for years seemed to have fallen away. He was at a ranch where people knew and didn't care that he was gay; he'd met a guy who liked him and was open about it. Hell, he was talking to horses again and fucking happy. It really didn't get much better than that. Brian left the barn and continued smiling all the way to the bunkhouse. David was dressed and waiting for him at the bunkhouse table, which had been cleaned, along with the kitchen. Apparently David was getting stir-crazy enough for housework.

"Are you ready to go?"

"God, yes. I want out of this place for a few hours," David said with a smile and began pulling on his coat.

"Okay. Give me just a few minutes to shower and change. I smell like the barn. I won't be long, and then we can go, I promise." Brian hurried to his room and grabbed the clothes he'd laid out. Then he rushed to the bathroom and showered in record time, ignoring his dick, which seemed to point in David's general direction no matter what he did. Once he was done, he dried off and dressed quickly. His hair was still a little wet when he joined David in the living area, ready to go.

David took one look at him and smiled. Then he walked up to Brian and placed his hat on his head. "I don't want you to get cold." How that would be possible in the glow of David's warmth was beyond him.

They left the bunkhouse and walked to where Brian's car sat covered in a heap of snow. It took a while to dig it out and scrape the windows. But once inside, the engine turned right over, and they started the trip to town.

The one good thing about the old car was that the heater cranked. It wasn't long before they were toasty warm. David turned on the radio, and Willie Meadows' latest hit filled the car. The drive seemed almost too short, and Brian thought about making a few wrong turns, but he needed gas and filled the tank at the station before getting lucky enough to find a parking space in front of the diner downtown.

Brian was all smiles as they went inside.

"You can sit anywhere," one of the servers said as he hustled past.

They found an empty table near the door and sat down. A waitress passed out menus and took their drink orders before hurrying away again. The place was definitely hopping, and it looked like half the town had decided to have lunch there.

"The food here is really good," David said and opened his menu.

Brian did the same and looked it over before quickly deciding on the turkey dinner.

The waitress returned and sighed slightly. "Morning, sugars, do you know what you'd like?" She was a little out of breath. Thankfully for her, it looked like some tables were emptying and not being refilled with customers, so maybe the lunch rush would be coming to an end soon. Brian ordered, and David decided to have the same thing. "So how are things? You work out at the Holden place, right? You guys getting dug out?"

"We sure are. I hope this weather holds a little while longer. It would be nice to melt some of the snow," David said.

She smiled and leaned on the table slightly. "That it would. All of us are about sick of it." She seemed to be settling in for a spell. "I hear you got a new hand out there. Someone who used to work at the Flying C."

"Yes," Brian said, and she seemed to remember he was there. All her attention had been focused on David, and Brian stifled his grin when he realized she'd been flirting a little. "They were good enough to take me in when I needed a place."

She seemed surprised, and the relaxed posture she'd taken on disappeared almost instantly. "That's mighty good of them," she said and hurried away. Brian stared after her and then looked at David, wondering what in the hell had just happened.

"That was strange," Brian observed. "Maybe she just realized her flirting wasn't going to get her anywhere." Even as he said the words, a black void of worry crept up inside him.

A swell of laughter went up from toward the back of the restaurant, and David turned toward the sound. Brian followed his gaze and swallowed hard. Rocklin sat with a bunch of the hands from the Flying C. This was not going to be good. All he wanted to do was leave and go back to the ranch, but he wasn't a coward, and he hoped they wouldn't pull anything here.

"Do you know them?" David asked.

"Yeah. The big guy with his back to us, with the long black hair, is Rocklin. With his buddies from the Flying C." They didn't usually come this far. The Flying C was closer to Hobart and the men usually went there, so Brian hadn't been expecting to see them.

"The ones that got you fired?" David asked and Brian nodded. "They better not try anything here."

"They probably won't." Brian hoped he was right. They weren't the kind of men to cause trouble outright. They were the kind who would go behind a guy's back and sabotage his work… and worse… in order to make him look bad. Brian watched them get up and knew the instant they saw him. Their smiles turned to sneers, especially Rocklin's. But they said nothing and filed past the table without making a single comment. If looks could kill, Brian would have been six feet under, but once the door closed behind them, he began to breathe again.

The waitress brought their plates and she seemed subdued. It looked to Brian as though she was trying to get David's attention, but he wasn't paying her any mind, and once the food was set and their coffee refilled, she left. "What was that about?"

David shrugged. "Sometimes folks are strange," he commented softly before beginning to eat. Brian picked up his fork as well and noticed that people were looking at him. Not overtly, but when he turned their way, they seemed to shift their gazes. David didn't seem to notice, and the looks tapered off. Brian figured he'd been imagining things and went back to his lunch, which was excellent.

Brian was stuffed by the time he finished. He set down his fork and leaned back in his chair. "That was wonderful," Brian told the waitress when she returned. "Thank you."

Some of her frost melted and she gave him a smile as she picked up his wiped-clean plate. "You're welcome, sugar." She took David's plate as well, asked if they wanted dessert, and then left the check. Brian reached for it, but David got to it first. He scowled, but David just grinned, and Brian excused himself to go to the restroom.

When he came out, he saw David at the register paying the bill. He stopped at the table and picked up his coat, along with David's hat, and joined him. David finished as he approached, and they left the diner, then paused on the sidewalk. "Do you want to walk?" Brian asked. "The theater is just down the street."

David paused and then turned toward him. "That's fine." They started down the sidewalk, and Brian shoved his hands in his pockets to keep them warm. Other people were going inside the theater already, and they joined the small procession at the box office. Brian hoped Rocklin and his friends weren't there. The last thing he needed was trouble. He'd been so happy, but now David looked tense and a little grim.

"Would you rather go back to the ranch? Is your ankle hurting?"

"I'm fine," David said lightly, and they bought tickets and went into the old theater.

It felt like stepping back in time. The art deco snack bar looked like it hadn't changed at all in many decades. Whoever owned the theater took good care of it. The walls were clean and the paint seemed fresh. Brian got popcorn for the two of them, because it wasn't a movie without popcorn, and they went inside.

The seats were old, but had been well maintained. They found a pair and sat down. Brian looked around and was relieved to see that Rocklin and his friends weren't there.

"Are you okay?" David asked.

"Yeah," Brian said. "I just don't want any trouble, that's all."

"You mean from the other guys," David said.

"Yeah. They sabotaged my work, and Rocklin is a huge closet case. He'll do anything to keep his little secret quiet." Now that he had some distance from the situation, he thought it seemed completely stupid to hide who you were. Brian was much happier being out and open than he'd ever been in the closet, sneaking around.

David nodded, but didn't say anything more. He still looked worried, and Brian wondered what that was about. They had been all fun and smiles on the way over. Something was going on. He turned to David to ask about it, but the trailers started and David seemed intent on watching the screen.

The movie was intense, but great, with explosions big and bright enough that Brian swore a few times he could feel the heat. As the credits began to roll, they got up to leave and put on their coats. Brian carried the trash and dumped it in one of the cans on the way out. The sun was getting low in the sky as they walked down the sidewalk back toward the car. David didn't say much.

"What's going on? You've been really quiet."

David stopped as they approached the car. "You let Haven and Dakota hire you without telling them the whole story about why you got fired. You should have said something."

"I did. The guys sabotaged my work, I told you that. I've been here for almost two weeks, and you know I work hard. So does Haven."

"Not that." David turned around. "People are saying that you were fired for stealing."

"I was. But I never took anything. Like I said, the men wanted to get rid of me, and the boss was happy with my work." Brian's pulse quickened and his stomach clenched. He should have known this would come up, and David was right; he should have said something. But how could he? No one would hire him if they found out, and he'd been desperate. Besides, it wasn't true.

"I never stole things from anyone. Some of the men started complaining that things were missing. They decided to search my room, and lo and behold, there was all the stuff. How convenient for them." Brian glared daggers at David. "I never took what wasn't mine." Brian unlocked his door and yanked it open. "What I can't believe is that you actually believed it. You saved my life and I saved yours. Hell, I was beginning…. Oh, screw it. I should have known it was too good to be true." He got in and pulled the door closed with a heavy thud, then started the engine. David got in the passenger seat and sat as rigid as a board as he fastened his seat belt.

Brian fumed and put the car in gear, then drove back out toward the ranch, gripping the wheel so tightly his knuckles were white. He refused to glance over at David, and after he pulled into the drive and parked the car, he got out and walked directly to the bunkhouse. It hurt like hell that David had believed the lies spread by people who'd wanted to get rid of him. Fuck, David hadn't asked him about it; he'd just demanded to know why Brian hadn't told them he was a thief. He wasn't a thief. Okay, maybe when he was a kid he'd taken a nickel from his mother's purse once for candy, but other than that, he'd never….

"What's going on?" Gus asked as Brian passed through the living area.

"Why don't you ask David? He can bring you up to date on the latest gossip." Brian didn't slow his pace for a second until he was in his room and had closed the door.

His anger lasted for a good thirty minutes and then shifted to fear and recrimination. He should have told them more of what happened, but he was ashamed. To be accused of stealing… that had hurt, but to have them find supposed proof of it in his room…. The kind of hatred it took to do something like that chilled Brian to the core. He never wanted to encounter anything like that again in his life. He punched the mattress because he realized he'd screwed up.

He wondered if he should simply pack his things and go. If David believed the rumors and lies, then everyone else most likely would as well. He could explain what truly happened until he was blue in the face, but no one would believe him.

"Brian," David said softly from outside his door.

"Go away," he called back without getting up. "I think you've said enough already."

"Brian, I...."

Brian reached over to the side of the bed and hit the button on the old clock to start the radio. He didn't need to listen to David's excuses or how he wanted Brian to hear his side of things. David should have asked him and not done the same thing the others had done and accuse him of being a thief. *Fuck, what am I going to do now?*

Leaving seemed like the only option. He'd been heading out of town to try to get some distance from the Flying C when he'd run off the road and ended up here. He figured he might as well pack up and continue that journey, put as much distance between himself and the problem as he could. The only thing was, he couldn't run away from the real problem: people thinking he was a thief. There was no getting away from that because even people he cared about didn't believe in him. All he could do was hide and be as careful as possible.

He looked around the room. He had thought he'd found an ideal place. People here didn't care that he was gay. Well, it didn't matter. No one wanted to work with a thief.

Chapter Six

DAVID KNEW he'd messed up, big-time, as he walked back down the hall from Brian's room. He should have asked him about what he'd heard at the diner. Just because the woman at the drugstore had hinted at a similar thing and then their server had tipped him off about what was being said, he shouldn't have believed it… but he had. David had barely seen anything of the movie. For two hours he'd ruminated and gotten angrier and angrier, convincing himself that Brian had lied to all of them. Maybe he had and maybe he hadn't, but David should have asked him about it.

"What did you do?" Gus snapped in a whisper as soon as David flopped down in one of the chairs.

"I found out why he was fired from the Flying C, and…."

"The bullshit about him stealing?" Gus asked, and David swallowed hard. "Yeah, I heard that days ago, and so did Phillip when I rode into town with him. Neither of us believed it, so Phillip called out there, and the Wagoners told him that they figured out what was going on after Brian had been let go and they regret it." Gus looked down the hallway. "That boy was picked on and abused by those people, and now he got the same thing from you."

"You already knew?" David said and swallowed hard.

"Yes. And it wasn't true, not one little bit." Gus scowled at him. "Do you think a thief would have stayed with you when you'd gotten hurt and taken care to make sure you were warm enough? Hell, no. A thief would probably have hurried back to the ranch to get help and left you there. Someone that self-centered and selfish would have hauled ass so fast it would have made your head spin." Gus shook his head. "Brian has a good heart, and I think he had it set on you, but I don't know what I'd do now if I were him."

"Shit…," David swore softly and stood up again. He hurried down the hall to Brian's room and knocked again, but got no answer. He tried the door: locked. David knocked again, but Brian still didn't answer. He went back into the living area and sat back down, not knowing what in the hell he should do. He sat and stared at the television for a long time and then realized what he had to do… and who he needed to talk to.

He jumped up and hurried outside, climbed in his truck, and drove to Wally and Dakota's. It was already dark by the time he arrived. David parked off to the side and walked down the snow-covered path to the foreman's house. He knew the way by heart and the journey he was making tugged at his heart as he trod the familiar path.

He stopped outside the door. He wasn't sure if this was a good idea, but he was already there. Hell, it might be one of the worst ideas he'd ever had. But it felt right, and like something he had to do. Holding his breath, he knocked on the door. Footsteps sounded from inside and then the door opened.

Gordon looked out at him and scowled. "Yes?" he asked.

David had never heard one word convey so much freaking power before.

David felt like he was ten years old, going over to a friend's house to ask if he could come out and play. "I'd like to speak with Mario, please."

Gordon didn't move at first, but then he slowly stepped back. David entered, and Gordon closed the door behind him. "Have a seat," Gordon said, pointing to one of the kitchen chairs. "I'll see if he wants to talk to you." That Gordon doubted he would didn't need to be said—it was clear in his tone.

David sat down and watched Gordon leave. The house looked much the same as when he'd lived there with Mario, except not. Things were different. The furniture was the same and the walls were the same color, but the feel was different. It was warmer and homier. Happier. And it hurt.

"What do you need?" Mario snapped as he came into the kitchen.

"I just want to talk," David said as gently and sincerely as he possibly could. His instinct was to piggyback on Mario's hostility, but he forced himself not to.

"The last time we talked, it took me hours to get Gordon to speak to me again, and he's still hurt. So why should I bother?"

"Because I was wrong. I see that now. I caused you pain and I went about things all wrong. I should have tried to work things out, and yeah, things hadn't been good between us, but I shouldn't have run around behind your back. I know you think I was unfaithful, but I wasn't. At least not physically. I didn't do anything with anyone while we were together. But that didn't stop me from pulling away from you, and…. Anyway, I was wrong. I should have dealt with things head-on instead of running away like I did. It hurt you and I hurt myself."

Mario's expression softened. "What brought this on?"

"I had my eyes opened, I guess. I screwed things up but good with Brian today, and it made me realize how I'd messed things up with you."

Mario nodded.

Gordon came into the kitchen and said, "I'll leave the two of you to talk since it doesn't look like you're going to be ripping each other to shreds." There was still a warning in Gordon's expression and voice. He lightly touched Mario's shoulder and then left.

"We both know that everything is not your fault, no matter how much and how long I blamed you. We were growing apart, and that's hard for anyone. I didn't want to see it because I thought we were happy, and then when you left, I felt as though you tore the happiness away."

"But it was an illusion," David said. "For both of us."

Mario sighed. "Yes, it was. But popping that bubble the way you did was not right. I guess I'm saying things between us could have been ended better. And if you'd just stayed away, I could have gone on hating you and blaming you for everything, but you didn't. You came back because you felt you'd made a mistake."

David nodded.

"The only mistake you made was the way things ended," Mario said. "I think we both see that now."

"I think we do," David agreed.

"But you're still running, aren't you?" Mario challenged. "When things got tough, you ran. That was what hurt the most."

"I guess," David said. He wasn't sure what Mario was getting at.

"So what happened with Brian? Let me guess: you heard the rumors in town and figured where there was smoke, there's fire." Mario's gaze drilled into him. "Yes, we've all heard them, and they're not true. In fact, to most of us, it's old news."

"Yeah," David said, feeling like complete shit. "I heard the rumors and got angry because I thought he'd been playing everyone here."

Mario shook his head. "You have to be one of the worst judges of character of anyone I ever met."

"I think Gus told me the same thing."

"Knowing Gus, he probably did. So you jumped to conclusions and hurt Brian." Mario paused for a few seconds. "You need to stop this running. Because that's what you're doing, even if you don't see it. So there was a rumor going around town. It was started by people who don't like Brian and tried to get him run off. Why would anyone listen to it? We did, for about two seconds, and then we checked and proved it wrong. That was days ago, and the whole thing would have died away completely if you'd asked him or simply trusted that he wasn't that kind of person." Mario leaned forward. "You don't trust anyone, and when they disappoint you in some way, you bail fast. I suspect Brian has had a lot of people bail on him too, and now he can add you to the list."

David didn't want to hear that, but he knew it was the truth. "I think this is what I missed the most."

Mario sat back. "I don't understand."

"Okay," David began. "I left and I admit that. But it was never the same. I think I came back because I thought I still loved you, but maybe what I really missed was the friendship."

Mario nodded. "I can understand that. I did love you, but when you left, what I missed most was having you to talk to."

David nodded. "So what do I do? I really care for him, and I screwed up big-time." Mario flinched slightly. "I'm sorry. This is not meant to hurt you. I just don't want to make the same mistake."

"I know." Mario looked toward the living room. "I think it's time we both moved on and tried to get back to being friends again." Mario sighed slightly. "And as your friend, I'd say you need to talk to Brian… and listen to him. Let him tell you how he feels. You're the one who hurt him, so be prepared to work to build his trust again. If you really love him, then stop running away. Let him know you're willing to run toward him."

David nodded nervously and glanced at his watch. Brian was in the bunkhouse, hurting, and it was time he did something about it. "I need to get back, but…." David stood up and Mario did the same. Without thinking, David hugged him tight. "I really did miss you."

"I missed you too," Mario whispered. "Now go back to Brian and try to make things right."

David let go and strode toward the door. He turned back to Mario and said, "Thank you." As he pulled open the door, he saw Gordon come into the room, but he didn't stop. He nearly tripped twice on his way to the truck because he didn't want to slow down. He got in the car and had the engine started almost before he'd pulled the door closed. Then he turned around and barreled out of the drive, relieved that the roads were clear, because his foot seemed like it was made of lead. The rear tires slipped slightly when he made the turn into the drive at home, and he slid to a stop outside the bunkhouse.

As soon as he got out, he looked for Brian's car and breathed a sigh of relief when he saw it still sitting where it had been. David got out and slammed the door, then rushed into the bunkhouse and down the hall to Brian's room. The door stood open, but the room was empty. "Do you know where Brian went?" he called over his shoulder. He went in and opened the closet door, confirming his worst fear: it was bare. David closed the door and hurried back the way he came. "Did Brian leave?"

Luke shrugged. "I just got in a few minutes ago and haven't seen him. Why?"

"His stuff is gone. I saw his car outside, but his room looks like it's been cleaned out." David realized Luke didn't know crap and raced back outside. Brian's car was still parked outside. He hurried over to it and peered in the windows. Bags and clothes were piled on the backseat. Brian was leaving, that much was clear, but where was he now?" David looked all around the car. Multiple sets of footprints had tamped down the snow, so that was no help.

He heard the door of the main house open and looked up, hoping like hell it was Brian. He had to find him and stop him. He needed to tell him he'd been a stupid fool and got ready to grovel. "Have you seen Brian?" he asked Phillip when he came out onto the porch.

"Not in the last little while, no. Have you checked the barn?" Phillip descended the stairs to the drive.

"No. His closet is empty and the car is full of his things."

"He's leaving?" Phillip hurried over and pulled open the car door, shining the dome light on the contents. "What happened? I thought he was happy here."

"I screwed up and hurt him. I didn't mean to. I heard the rumors in town and jumped to conclusions."

Phillip closed the car door. "You should have known better. The rest of us did. He was set up. It was obvious to us." Phillip glared at him in the light reflected off the snow. "You're the one who should have taken his side above all. No wonder he thought about leaving. After all, if you didn't believe in him, why should anyone else?"

"Did he know you knew?"

"No. We heard it, didn't believe it, and then confirmed it. End of story. No need to upset him with a bunch of bullshit cooked up by a group of vindictive, closed-minded, bigoted ranch hands." Little bits of spittle flew as Phillip ground out the words.

"I need to find him." David turned and hurried toward the barn. He said a silent prayer that Brian was inside saying goodbye to the horses. He pushed open the door, expecting to see Brian near one of the stalls. All he heard were horses shifting in their stalls and the nails of the dogs on the concrete as they trotted over to see what was going on. He heard footsteps behind him. "He's not here."

"I can see that." Phillip strode by him, peered into each stall, and then pulled open the tack room door.

"What the hell is going on?" David asked under his breath. "He didn't go into town with the guys. His car is still here. I mean, if he'd left, the car would be gone. It's obvious he was getting ready to leave, but he isn't here and he isn't gone either."

"I know. Come on." Phillip strode out of the barn. David followed, closing the door in a rush and then following Phillip across the yard and around the house. A lone set of footprints led off across the yard toward the fence line. Phillip began running, with David right behind, as fast as his still tender ankle would allow. They followed the trail along the fence posts and then between the pastures, back toward the creek that ran along the northern edge of the property.

"Why would he come back here at this time of night?" David wished he had a flashlight, but the moon was out and it was full, casting enough light on the snow-covered land to see the basic outlines. There were shadows everywhere, however, and a flashlight would have done wonders.

"Maybe he needed to think." Phillip didn't slow down for a second. "Haven and I used to come back here all the time. There's a log and a boulder near the creek where he and I used to sit when we wanted to be alone. It became our spot."

"Is that where you think Brian is?" David hurried as Phillip sped up.

"It's possible. Haven may have pointed out the spot at some point. It certainly looks like that's where this trail is leading us."

The snow was wet and heavy after melting under three days of sun. David's shoes were nearly soaked, but he ignored the chill and kept moving. If it meant finding Brian, he'd put up with an aching ankle and cold feet.

As they proceeded, David heard water. It was usually a large stream, but he realized he was hearing it from quite a distance. The water must be high and flowing fast. The sound got steadily louder and louder. "Brian," David called and waited for some response. He heard nothing as they approached the string of trees that lined the creek. As dark as it was, they didn't dare go any farther. The light from the moon didn't penetrate the trees, and they had no way of knowing how high the water was. It sounded like it was right nearby.

"Brian," Phillip called. "Are you there?"

A muffled cry and a shuffle reached David's ears, and he pointed. "Over there," he yelled and took off. He followed the trees, carefully snaking around them. "Brian," he cried and listened again. Phillip was right behind him, standing stock-still. David saw something ahead of him running away on all fours. He couldn't tell what it was, only the movement at the edge of the darkness and then it was gone. Only the snap of twigs told him he hadn't imagined the whole thing.

A soft shuffling from just off to his left made David turn, and he veered off and headed in that direction, his heart pounding in his ears. If Brian was out there, what was David going to find?

"What in hell was that?" Phillip sounded breathless.

"I think it was a wolf," David said as he peered into the dark. A little ways ahead, Brian lay on his side in the snow. David raced over to him and skidded to a halt, his knees giving out. Brian appeared to be moving, trying to get up. "Are you okay?" David asked.

Brian lifted his head and tried to get up. "David," Brian gasped and struggled to his feet.

"I'm calling for help," Phillip said, and seconds later he was issuing orders and telling people to get out here as fast as they could.

"Are you hurt?" David began patting him down and then pulled him to him. "Jesus, what the hell happened? What were you doing out here when it's getting dark?" David wasted no time and held Brian to try to warm him. Brian's clothes were soaked and he'd started to shiver.

"I feel so stupid. I decided to take a walk. Haven had told me there was a spot out here where he and Phillip used to go, and I got it in my head to try to find it. I figured all I had to do was follow the fence line." Brian swore softly. "I was so stupid and upset. I got to the top of the berm, lost my balance, slid down this side, and banged my head on a tree. I had a flashlight, but I lost it when I fell. I was trying to find it and heard you calling."

"I didn't hear you answer. We were looking for you. I was scared half to death, and we saw...." David stopped. There was no need to add additional drama to the moment. "Phillip, please tell them we need blankets and—"

"I already did. Dakota said they were on their way."

The whine of snowmobiles split the quiet and lights shone as the first vehicle crested the berm and slid down the side. Phillip waved his cell phone so Dakota and the others could see the light, and Dakota carefully made his way through the trees.

"What happened?" Dakota demanded as he got off the snowmobile and hurried over. He began wrapping Brian in blankets.

"I'm fine, just stupid," Brian said, pulling the blanket around his shoulders as he moved toward Dakota's snowmobile.

David followed as a second machine crested the berm and pulled up beside the first.

"Let's get him back to the house," Dakota said. David recognized Gordon as he got closer. A third snowmobile joined them. Dakota got Brian on his snowmobile, and Phillip climbed on with Gordon. David got on the back of the third, driven by Wally, and they all took off like bats out of hell.

David's teeth should have been chattering, but he was so angry and upset that he didn't feel the cold. How could Brian do this? It made no sense to him. Brian had impressed him as being clearheaded and thoughtful under pressure. This just didn't seem like him at all.

"You don't have to squeeze that hard," Wally said, slowing down. "I'll get you back, and Brian is going to be fine." David loosened his hold, and Wally sped up.

They arrived at Haven and Phillip's a few minutes later. What had seemed to take forever on foot was covered by the snowmobiles in just a few minutes. As soon as they rounded the main house and pulled to a stop next to the others, David jumped off and hurried inside. Brian sat in one of the chairs, the blanket pulled tightly around him. "What...," David began and then stopped himself. He was shaking slightly. "What were you thinking?"

Dakota and Gordon came in from the kitchen, with Phillip and Haven right behind them. David swallowed hard and backed away as Wally joined them from outside.

"I want to take a look at your head," Dakota said to Brian. David got out of the way. He wasn't going to get any answers now. He wanted to ask Brian his questions without everyone else around, but that didn't seem likely anytime soon. Dakota checked Brian's vision and balance. He asked a bunch of questions about whether Brian had blacked out. He said he hadn't, and David was relieved to hear that.

"I was just a little disoriented for a minute or so. Then Phillip and David found me. I had decided to come back before I took the tumble down the berm."

Dakota asked him to stand, then walk. Brian seemed steady on his feet, and his eyes looked clear. That sent a wave of relief through David.

"I want you to take it easy for the rest of the night and let me know right away if you start to feel ill or dizzy at all," Dakota said.

"I will," Brian promised and then stood up. "I think I've caused enough trouble for all of you." Brian's gaze settled on Phillip and Haven.

"We'll head out," Dakota said and shared a look with Wally and Gordon. The three of them left the house, and soon the whine of the snowmobiles sounded outside, then quickly faded into the distance.

"David, I think you should head back to the bunkhouse." Haven stepped forward and sat on the sofa near Brian, with Phillip sitting next to him. David was obviously being dismissed, so he turned and left the house, then walked across the yard to the bunkhouse.

The other men all looked up as he came in. David did his best to ignore them and went straight to his room. He and Brian really needed to talk. He only hoped he got the chance.

The guys called him for dinner a few minutes later. David joined them and ate a little, but he wasn't hungry. He kept staring at the door, hoping Brian would come in. After dinner, he helped clean up and then went outside. Brian's car was still parked out front, so at least he knew he hadn't left. That didn't mean he wasn't going to, though. David went back inside and sat with the guys watching television. He had no idea what they watched, and he really didn't care. All he could think about was Brian out there alone. Yeah, he'd said he'd gone out there to think, but there had to be more to it than that. David's mind conjured up all kinds of scenarios, and most of them ended badly.

"Is Brian okay?" Gus asked at one point.

David nodded and sank a little lower into his misery. "Dakota checked him over. When I was out there I think I might have seen a wolf, or at least a wild dog." He said the words but there was no feeling in them.

"I think I saw him earlier today. It looked like a feral dog to me. It didn't have that wolf gait or shape, but I only saw him for a second."

David nodded slightly. "I only saw him in the dark, but I thought I should let someone know." He turned his attention back to the television, but didn't really see it. "Brian is going to be okay," he said under his breath to try to reassure himself.

"Where is he?" As Gus asked the question, the bunkhouse door opened and Brian came in, carrying a single bag. He smiled at the guys and said hello, but went straight through to his room and closed the door. David stared after him and wondered if he should go talk to him—if Brian would want to talk to him. He glanced at Gus and then stood up. It was time he stopped being a wuss and listened to Mario's advice. If he wanted Brian in his life, then he needed to show him that he truly cared.

He took a deep breath, walked down the hall, and knocked softly on the door. He expected to be told to go away, but he'd already decided he wasn't going to take that for an answer. "Brian, it's me."

The door opened and David went inside. He closed the door and turned to Brian, pulled him into his arms, and kissed him, releasing all the fear and anxiety that had built up over the past few hours. Brian stiffened at first but then returned the kiss.

"You had me so scared," David whispered when he broke the kiss. "I know I screwed up. I shouldn't have assumed the rumors were true." He tugged Brian closer. "I went to talk to Mario. After what I did to you, I had an epiphany of sorts. I realized some things and I needed to talk to him. He told me a lot of things I didn't want to hear, but needed to listen to anyway."

Brian stared at him, openmouthed. "You went to see Mario?"

"Yeah, I know it sounds dumb, but we were together for three years and... I needed to talk to someone I trusted. Even though we haven't seen eye to eye on things, I still trust him. Anyway, he brought a great deal of clarity to what I'd done to you and what I'd done to him." David held Brian closer. "I've been such an ass to everyone important in my life."

"So you and Mario worked things out?"

"I think we started to, yeah. It will never be like it was, and that's okay. Our relationship, other than maybe as friends, has been over for a long time. But he's a good friend and he opened my eyes to the way I've been acting. Including the fact that I need to start trusting the people I want in my life. I haven't been doing that, and that starts with you. If you'll have me."

"I should have told you all of what happened." Brian rested his head on David's shoulder. "I knew I hadn't taken anything, and it killed me that they accused me of it and that the bosses believed it. They fired me, and then I didn't think anyone would believe me."

"And the way I acted just reinforced that." David closed his eyes. He'd wanted to kick himself so many times over the past few hours. "And none of it was necessary. Haven and Dakota already knew, and Phillip apparently called the Flying C and got to the bottom of things. You were set up, just like you said. From what I heard, the Wagoners were not particularly happy."

"They are good people. But I know it would be hard for anyone to discount evidence like what the men concocted." Brian stepped back and smiled slightly.

"Well, that may be, but I shouldn't have listened to those rumors. I should have asked you what happened and not believed those damn rumors." David opened his mouth to explain what he'd been thinking but then closed it again. He had no excuse and he wasn't going to offer one. He could still see the hurt on Brian's face when he'd confronted him. That was an expression he never wanted to see again. The thought of it stabbed David in the heart and made his chest ache. "Do you think you can forgive me?"

Brian smiled and nodded. "I already have. That's why I went for that walk. I needed to think things through, and I figured if I had been honest with everyone about what had happened…."

"Maybe we both need to talk to each other," David suggested and tugged Brian into another kiss. He feasted on Brian's lips, lightly tracing the outline of Brian's lips with his tongue. He was so damned relieved he couldn't put it into words. He cupped Brian's cheeks, stroking over the day's growth with his thumbs. "When I got back and saw that you'd packed everything, I could hardly breathe. Were you really going to leave?"

"That's part of what I needed to think about. I don't want to leave. This place feels like home. The people are good and they understand who I am. I don't have to hide. Yet, I wasn't sure I belonged. If everyone thought I was a thief, then no one would trust me and there was no way I could stay. You know that working on a ranch requires trust. We work alone and in small groups for much of the time. If you can't trust your men, then as a rancher, you have to let them go, and if you can't trust the men you work with, then you're constantly looking over your shoulder instead of getting the job done. You know that."

"Yeah, I do. But you are trustworthy and did nothing wrong. Don't ever run because of what others think of you. I made that mistake more than once, but I won't again." David hardened his expression to emphasize his conviction.

"Are you still in love with Mario?"

"No," David answered flatly. "I haven't been in quite a while. When I first came back, I was a real mess. Everything had fallen apart and I thought I still was, or maybe I just wanted to believe I was because if he and I were together again, he would help me pick up the pieces. I know now that if he'd have taken me back, we both would have been miserable." David turned to Brian. "But I am in love. I know that." He leaned forward and then stopped, waiting for Brian to come the rest of the way. He slid his eyes closed, but Brian didn't move at all.

"David," he whispered.

David opened his eyes. Brian gaped at him. "Yes. I love you," David said. "I knew that as soon as I thought you might be gone. I knew I'd messed up and wanted a chance to make it right. The thought of you leaving and me never seeing you again scared the shit out of me. I'll understand if you don't feel the same, and I don't expect you to say the words just because I said them. I messed up, and—" David stopped and held Brian tighter.

"You know we're cowboys, not little girls," Brian chortled and then broke into a fit of laughter. "Listen to us, talking about our feelings and crap."

David began to laugh as well, but it quickly died away. "Maybe it's being around the others here at the ranch, but I want you to know how I feel. And I want you to be happy." He lightly brushed his hand through Brian's hair, then cupped the back of his head and drew him in.

The kiss started soft, but quickly built. Brian maneuvered them over to the bed and pressed David down onto it, then stood between David's legs, kissing him all the while. David hadn't meant for this to turn into sex, he really hadn't. All he had been hoping for was the chance to talk. However, from the way Brian was kissing him, further talk was definitely off the table. David went from zero to sixty in about two seconds and pulled Brian down onto the bed. He scooted them back, and once he was comfortable, he began tugging at Brian's shirt.

They parted just long enough for David to get the shirt over Brian's head. Then Brian tugged and nibbled at his lips while David stroked down Brian's smooth sides. God, his skin felt like heaven, like coming home.

"What was that little growl for?" Brian asked, his breath ghosting over David's lips.

"Just that I want you to be mine for always. I know I have no right to want that right now, but I do." He closed his eyes and let his hands feast on Brian's back, splaying his fingers so he could touch as much of him as he could. "You're who I want to go to sleep with and wake up next to. I don't want you to go anywhere unless it's with me." David kissed him. "I love you, Brian. I think I always have."

They locked gazes in that second, and David saw his own feelings reflected back. Brian might not have been ready to say the words, but the heat and intensity present in his eyes were enough for now. David knew he needed to show Brian that he could trust him with his heart, and that wouldn't come from words, but from actions and time. He drew Brian closer, parted his lips slightly, and then covered Brian's lips with his own.

Their clothes ended up on the floor with delicious slowness. The air between them crackled with excitement, but neither of them seemed in a hurry. David wanted to savor every second with Brian and listen to every tiny sound, from the slight hum when he sucked on his ear to the moan that escaped when David licked around Brian's nipple with just the tip of his tongue. He adored the musky, outdoor taste of Brian's skin and didn't waste a single opportunity to get more. He stilled for a second when he realized just how close he'd come to losing this forever, but then he pushed it aside. He had Brian with him, here and now, and he was going to make the very most of that opportunity.

Brian sat up, straddling his hips, and David reached out to lightly trace the tips of his fingers over Brian's chest and then down his belly. He gently stroked Brian's thighs and hips before cupping Brian's butt and slowly drawing him closer. He raised his head off the pillow, and as Brian neared, David sucked his cock between his lips. The unique flavor of the man he loved burst on his tongue. Brian moaned loudly, and David relished the sound as he took him deeper and sucked as hard as he could.

David shifted his gaze upward along Brian's work-built chest to his stubbled cheeks and wide, ecstatic eyes. Brian held the headboard, and David encouraged him to flex his hips. He wrapped his lips around Brian's thick cock and reveled in the way it slid over his tongue. Damn, that felt good, beyond good. Thought failed him, and David gave up trying to think. He simply delighted in the feeling.

He slid a finger alongside Brian's cock, wetting it, and then brought his finger to Brian's opening. He teased the skin and then slowly pressed inside. Brian gasped, stilled, and then thrust forward deeply. David pressed deeper and watched as Brian threw his head back. He growled low and deep in his throat. David bent his finger slightly, and Brian quaked like a leaf in the wind. It was one of the most beautiful sights David had ever experienced in his life.

"God, I… fuck… I can't…."

David simply hummed around Brian's cock, running his tongue along the base and around the head. Brian shook again and his cock throbbed and grew larger. David knew Brian was getting close, so he backed off, slowly removing his finger from Brian's body and gentling the sucking until Brian blew out a huge breath.

Brian pulled away and then kissed him hard. David took that opportunity to roll them on the bed, covering Brian with his body, pressing him into the mattress, chest to chest, lips to lips, cock to cock. Brian flexed his hips slightly, and David moved with him for a few seconds. Then he slowly slid down his body, licking and kissing his way down Brian's neck, across his chest, stopping to suck each nipple, and then down his belly, tracing the lines of muscle with his tongue before following the light treasure trail to Brian's cock. He sucked him in deeply again as he settled between Brian's legs.

Without stopping, David lifted Brian's legs and gently pressed them to his chest. Brian quivered slightly as David took him to the root and then let him slip from between his lips.

David slowly licked down Brian's crease, teasing the supersensitive skin, listening as Brian held his breath. He circled the small pink opening with a finger and then his tongue, delighting in Brian's intense taste. "Is this what you want?"

Brian nodded and gasped when David circled the puckered skin with his tongue and then pressed hard, licking the throbbing flesh and then up to Brian's balls. He sucked each into his mouth in turn before licking up his cock and sucking him in. Then he repeated the process in reverse, taking his time, loving every whine that Brian made along with each quiver of his strong body.

"Yes," Brian whispered over and over again. He reached for his cock again and again, and each time David gently pushed his hand away. "I need to come...."

"Not yet," David whispered as he stopped and settled Brian back on the bed. Brian pulled David up and kissed and nibbled on his lips. He shook, and when David climbed on top of him, Brian wrapped his legs around David's hips.

"I need you to fuck me, now. Right the hell now," Brian rasped. David didn't have his stuff with him. Brian extended his hand toward the nightstand, and David pulled the drawer open with a shaking hand. It nearly ended up on the floor before he found what be needed.

David lubed his fingers and pressed one and then another inside Brian's intense heat. Brian clenched his muscles around him so intensely that David swore his fingers went numb for a few seconds.

The energy between them was over the top. Every touch seemed intense. It didn't matter if it was Brian's hand on his chest, or the way he wrapped an arm around David's neck. Wherever Brian touched him came alive with extreme sensitivity. David twisted his fingers, making sure Brian was ready for him. When he pulled them away, Brian whimpered softly.

Somehow David managed to get the condom rolled on. His hands shook the entire time, but he rolled it on and got into place. He kissed Brian and positioned his cock at his opening, but didn't move yet. He could feel the throbbing of Brian's body, and when Brian sucked on David's tongue, he pressed forward.

Brian's body opened to him, gripping him as he slid into the tightest heat on earth. Nothing compared to this, and he realized nothing ever would again. Brian arched his back and gasped as the pressure slid further and further down David's cock. David heaved a gasping breath and stopped to give Brian a chance to catch his breath as well. His back ached for him to continue, to flex his hips and bury himself in Brian's body, but he overrode his instinct and held firm. He did not want to cause Brian any pain. This had to be all about pleasure. Then, when Brian relaxed around him, David pushed deeper until his hips rested against Brian's butt.

He stopped once again, his cock jumping slightly inside Brian's body. Brian sighed and held him tightly. They kissed and David pressed as deep inside Brian as he could, holding still. Then he slowly began to move.

David pulled away and then slowly moved back inside. Brian gasped quietly, and David's mouth fell open. The sensation of tight heat was nearly overwhelming. David caressed Brian's cheek and down his neck, needing as much contact as possible. "I love you," he whispered into Brian's ear.

David stroked slow and deep, rolling his hips and listening to Brian's breathing. When Brian panted, he slowed down slightly, and when he took deep, cleansing breaths, he stroked in time, in and out... in and out. That was all he needed. Brian's breathing told him everything he needed to know. The smallest change and David increased or decreased his tempo, holding Brian on the edge for as long as he possibly could. Brian's quivers and shakes increased as tension and erotic energy built between them. He stroked up Brian's sides to his arms, stretching them over Brian's head as he increased his pace slightly. "Trust me, Brian," David whispered.

Brian's breath caught in small hitches that increased in frequency. David increased his pace, locking gazes with Brian as they climbed the heights of passion together. The train was approaching the summit, and there was no stopping it now. David released Brian's arms and lifted himself up slightly, balancing on one hand as he wrapped the fingers of the other around Brian's cock.

His strokes weren't as smooth as he'd have liked, but Brian met them with vigor, pushing into his fist each time David pressed into him. The bed shook as David picked up speed, driving deeply into Brian.

They were lost in their own world and it was perfect. David didn't know how much longer he could hold out, but he was determined not to climax until Brian had. His toes and legs tingled, his arm shook, and his head throbbed. Brian clenched around him and his cock jumped in David's hand. With a whimpery cry, Brian rolled his head back and forth on the pillow as his body went rigid.

David felt the instant Brian reached his climax and his own followed right behind it. He remembered little after those first few seconds. His mind seemed to leave him and float next to Brian's on cottony clouds of pure delight. His only thought was that he wished he could stay there forever. Then slowly he descended and ended up on the bed, surrounded by Brian's warmth.

He held Brian close, keeping his eyes closed as he enjoyed just being held. He never wanted this moment to end. Their bodies separated, and David reluctantly stood up and took care of the condom. He used some tissues from the dispenser on the nightstand to clean them both up before crawling next to Brian and collapsing in wrung-out exhaustion. Brian moved closer, and David inhaled his warm scent with every breath. This was how he wanted to spend each night for the rest of his life—happy and wrapped in Brian's arms.

David shifted slightly, following the warmth of Brian's breath to his lips. They kissed gently and languidly, taking their time.

David remembered an old song about a man's love being in his kiss, and he hoped to hell the song was right.

Chapter Seven

BRIAN DIDN'T fall to sleep easily. He had the right to, and Lord knew he was tired enough to, but he couldn't. David had said he loved him. Brian wanted to believe it was true more than anything, but…. He reminded himself for what seemed like the millionth time that David was not like Rocklin. *He* would never have admitted he was wrong about anything. Rocklin was one of those men who felt every opinion he held was right, and if it turned out he might be wrong, Rocklin simply dug in his heels and wore out whoever was arguing with him or simply used his size to intimidate.

Rocklin had once told Brian that he loved him. Of course it turned out he'd said it to get something he wanted. And Brian had fallen for it big-time. He knew now that Rocklin had never loved him. All he'd really cared about was getting his rocks off on a regular basis and making sure Brian kept quiet about it. Everything else was a load of crap. Brian was pretty sure David meant what he'd said. But he needed some time to think, so he could be sure. He was in love with David, he knew that, but knowing it and saying it were two different things. And for Brian, those words were not to be said lightly.

"Go to sleep," David mumbled and pulled Brian closer. "I can hear you thinking. It will look clearer in the morning, I promise." David mumbled something else that Brian didn't understand. He closed his eyes and listened to David's soft breathing. Eventually it lulled him to sleep.

THE SUN shone brightly when he woke, its light streaming in the windows. Brian sat up and glanced at the clock before jumping out of bed. "David, we got chores to do and we're gonna be late." Things started early on the ranch and it was already almost seven. That was the official starting time for most of the men, and Brian took it very seriously. He began pulling on his clothes, and David hugged him from behind.

"It's all right," he breathed softly into Brian's ear. "Just get dressed and head on out. There are still people in the living room. I can hear their voices." David sucked on Brian's ear, and then work was the last thing he wanted.

"I'm not going to be able to walk out there in my jeans without everyone seeing what I got."

David held him tighter for a moment. "Sorry." Then he let Brian go and began gathering his clothes from the floor. He pulled on his jeans and carried the rest, leaving the room with a quick smile and closing the door behind him.

Brian finished dressing and headed to the bathroom to clean up. The other men were getting ready to head out when he came into the living room. He wolfed down a breakfast sandwich and grabbed one for David too. He waited for him, and when he appeared, Brian stuffed the sandwich in his hand before putting on his gear and heading out to the barn. He had plenty to do, and since it was nice, he put the horses out in their pastures with some hay and got down to work. The stalls were dirty, so he started at the far end of the barn and began cleaning. He shoveled out the stalls, emptied the water troughs, and removed the old hay. Then he put the stall back together, adding fresh water and hay as well as bedding before moving on to the next stall. He heard David at the other end of the barn.

They didn't talk, and Brian was grateful for that. He needed some time to think. He moved from stall to stall, doing his work, but not really giving it his full attention. After all these years working in barns and on ranches, it wasn't required. His body knew what needed to be done, which was a good thing, because Brian was unsettled, a little jittery, and damn if he could figure out why.

"Brian," David called softly from just outside the stall he was working in, and Brian jumped. He was lucky there was no horse in here with him—he would most likely have spooked it. "Sorry, I was just wondering where the smaller wheelbarrow was. The bigger ones are too heavy."

"It should be in the stall on the end that's empty. Haven said to use it for storage for now. He said in the spring we're going to have an equipment area added to the barn so we can organize things better, rather than storing it anywhere there's an inch of extra space."

"That will be nice. What has you so jumpy?" David asked from the other side of the wall and then stepped back in the doorway.

"I was just thinking, and I guess I wasn't paying that much attention to what was around me. With the horses outside, I let my mind wander and…."

"What are you thinking about so hard?" There was a worried edge to David's voice.

"It's not you," Brian said when the light went on. "I keep wondering how I could have let Rocklin treat me the way he did. I value myself more than that." Brian placed the shovel on the floor and leaned against the handle. "I'm a good cowboy and a hard worker. I know my way around a ranch and can do almost anything anyone asks me to. Over the years I've cared for more different kinds of animals than I can remember. I know when one is hurting and can care for most of them. There isn't anything here I can't do if I need to, short of veterinary surgery." Brian sighed. "So why would I let someone like Rocklin treat me like that?"

"You thought he cared for you," David offered. "Don't think for a minute that you're the only one who has been duped or fed a line of bull by a guy in order to get what he wants."

"Yeah, I know, but I should have been able to see through that."

"Do you think Rocklin really did care for you, but was too afraid to show it? I mean, look what the other men did to get rid of you. Maybe he thought they would do something like that to him too? I don't know, and I'm not justifying his behavior—I'm only trying to offer an explanation."

"You sound like you understand him," Brian said, and a cold draft crept up his neck. "Have you done something like that before?"

"I don't think so. When I was a kid I had to keep who I was a secret, but the guys I was with… we were just messing around. I kept work and sex separate. That is, until Mario. Then we got serious, and of course everyone here knew about us. But I understand Rocklin's fear. We've all felt it at one point." David stepped closer. "Think about it. You weren't open at the Flying C about who you were. People found out and then made your life hell."

Brian blinked. "That's true."

"Fear makes all of us do stupid things. I can tell you that from experience." David paused and took another step closer. "There's only one way you're ever going to get the answers you want, and that's to ask Rocklin. But I don't know if that's a good idea. We saw him at the diner yesterday. He barely looked at you. My guess is that he's so far in the closet it's ridiculous and you won't be able to get him alone."

"You're probably right, but I think I have to try."

David turned around and took about two steps before turning again. He looked like a nervous teenager pacing on a postage stamp. "I hate this. Look what they did to get rid of you. If you show up there again, who knows what those assholes will do to you."

Brian leaned the shovel against the side of the stall. "I have no intention of going there. If the Wagoners know that the men set me up, then there will definitely be no love lost for me because they will have made their displeasure known. I wasn't planning to go back. And you're right, I may never get a chance to talk to Rocklin, but what you said makes sense, and I can learn to live with that. I think I'll pretty much have to."

David moved closer and kissed him.

"What was that for?" Brian whispered.

"I just wanted you to know that I have your back. I don't want Rocklin or any of those guys from the Flying C anywhere near you."

"So now you're turning into Neanderthal Cowboy," Brian quipped.

"Just protective," David said softly. He hugged Brian one more time and then left the stall. Within a few minutes Brian heard the scrape of a shovel against the concrete and returned to work.

THE NEXT few days were blessedly quiet. The weather went from a mild thaw to cold again, which everyone around the ranch was relieved about. If it got too warm too fast, the snow would melt too quickly and the creek would flood. Haven had been monitoring it since the temperature rose, but with the cold and subsequent pause in the melting, the water level was going back down. David's ankle continued to heal and he stopped wearing the brace. He was able to do most of his normal work, but Brian did his best to make sure he did the heavier tasks.

Brian finished up his chores in the barn, glad he was done for the day. David had gone to Dakota and Wally's. Dakota had asked him to come over so he could look at his ankle, and David had called to say they needed some help there for the rest of the day. Brian told him he could finish up the work here, so they had worked apart. It almost seemed strange. For the past three days, they had worked together during the day and they'd spent the nights in Brian's bed. What surprised Brian most wasn't the way they made love as quietly as they could each night, but how quickly he had gotten used to sleeping with David. What bothered him was his inability to tell David how he felt. He'd come so close many times, but the words kept getting caught in his throat. He knew they shouldn't, because he did love David. He was strong and protective, and Brian had forgiven him for jumping to conclusions. It happened to everyone, and he wasn't going to punish David for it.

He sighed and checked each of the stalls before putting away all the tools. He closed the barn door and stepped out into the twilight. David's truck was parked next to his car, and Brian wondered how long he'd been back and why he hadn't joined him in the barn. As he walked to the bunkhouse, Luke met him coming the other way.

"Hey, Brian," Luke said with his usual clipped tone. "Phillip said for you to go to the main house."

"Thanks," Brian said. He turned around, hurried across the yard, and knocked on the front door. Phillip opened it and motioned him inside. Brian stepped into the living room and stopped dead in his tracks.

"Hi, Brian," Rocklin said as he stood up from one of the chairs. David stood next to him.

"We'll give the two of you a chance to talk. But Haven and I will be in the kitchen." Phillip took Haven's hand and led him out of the room.

"What are you doing here?" Brian asked, in total surprise.

Rocklin looked at David. "He showed up at the Flying C and put the screws to me." Rocklin twisted the brim of his hat. "Said you had things you wanted to ask me and then got in my face and asked if I was man enough to help fix what I'd screwed up." Rocklin looked more like a scared little boy than he did the confident, in-control guy Brian remembered.

Brian shifted his gaze to David and smiled. "Sit down," Brian said, and he walked further into the room and sat next to David on the sofa. "I have so many questions for you."

"But why didn't you come see me yourself?" Rocklin perched on the edge of the chair like he might jump up at any second.

"After what happened there? No." Brian did his best to keep his temper from rising. This was a time for level heads. "They put stuff in my room and then said I'd stolen it so they could get me fired, and they did it because I'm gay, just like you are. So, no, I don't have any intention of ever setting foot there again."

"I'm sorry about that. I didn't know they were going to do that," Rocklin said.

"That may be. But you didn't stand up for me either." Brian's resolve hardened. "You let that happen and said nothing. If you remember, when they said I was stealing stuff, I was with you. That was all you had to say, but you didn't. You let them succeed." Brian shifted forward. "I nearly died. I didn't have anywhere to go and I was out of money. It's winter, and no one is hiring. I damn near froze to death when my car went off the road." David slid his hand into Brian's. "David and the men here saved my life. They took me in, and even though they didn't really need another hand, they gave me a job and a place to live." He couldn't believe how fucking lucky he'd gotten. "At the lowest point in my life, I met some of the best people in the world."

Rocklin nodded. "Is that what you wanted to tell me?"

"Fuck, no," Brian exclaimed. "You said you cared for me, and I want to know if that was just a bunch of bullshit so you could get into my pants." Brian watched as Rocklin's cheeks colored. That told him all he needed to know. "Why would you do that to me? To anyone? Are you so far in the closet and so willing to hide who you are that you'll use and hurt the people around you?" Brian's heart pounded and he clenched his fists, squeezing David's hand.

"It was just sex. I thought you knew that. We were having a good time." Rocklin swallowed hard and paused. "At least I thought we were."

Brian scoffed loudly. "Yeah, right. Sneaking into the barn when no one was around or heading off and doing it in the cab of the truck when we were away from the ranch, yeah. That was a good time." His voice dripped with sarcasm. "I understood the need to keep things quiet. After all, we both needed the job. But, shit, Rocklin, you told me things. I know they were a bunch of crap, but dammit, you still said them." Brian stared at Rocklin and watched him squirm under the scrutiny.

Rocklin was well over two hundred pounds, tall and strong. The other men looked up to him because of his size and the way he could command a room. To see him flinch and act submissive was completely new, and it disturbed Brian a little. If Rocklin had blustered, he would have known he hadn't gotten through.

"Jesus Christ, you're just a scared little kid, aren't you?" Brian said. "You've got a secret and you're scared as hell the other men will find out you like dudes. Well, grow up. I know you didn't think enough of me to stand up to them. But you obviously didn't think enough of yourself either."

"That's not fair," Rocklin said forcefully. At last Brian was seeing some of the Rocklin he knew.

"Isn't it? You may not want to hear it, but it's true. You supposedly cared for me, but you let the men set me up, and you let them harass me until I had to leave. Was I nothing to you but someone to fuck?" Brian had his answer when Rocklin said nothing. God, how could he have ever thought Rocklin was worth the time of day? "Well, thank you for that."

"For what?" Rocklin snapped.

"Your silence speaks volumes." Brian looked at David and shifted slightly closer to him. "See, if you'd given a rat's ass about me, I might still be at the Flying C. Other than the Wagoners, that place is full of shit-kicking assholes. How such good people could hire such piles of crap is beyond me. But they did, and that's their problem."

"Those are good men," Rocklin said, jumping to his feet. He was trying to look powerful, but Brian now knew him for what he was and only saw the scared little boy inside.

"Yeah. They're so good, you're scared half to death they'll find out you're gay." Brian wasn't going to back down. He stood up as well and took a step toward Rocklin. "You can't intimidate me or anyone else here." Brian took a deep breath. "See, I'm grateful to you and all those assholes. If they hadn't done what they did, I would never have ended up here. This ranch"—Brian motioned all around him—"is filled with people-caring people. Haven and Phillip, Dakota and Wally—they own it and run it the way a ranch should be run."

"So everyone's a fag?" Rocklin said, and the last scale fell from Brian's eyes. Rocklin might like getting his cock sucked and fucking other guys, but he didn't see himself as gay, and that allowed him to delude himself. Why he hadn't thought of that sooner, Brian didn't know, but he understood in his heart it was true. And that revelation explained so much. He truly had been just someone to mess around with and help Rocklin get off.

"No. Not everyone is gay, and don't use that word around here if you want to get home in one piece. They don't tolerate the kind of attitude and behavior that they do at the Flying C. Everyone here is family. We care about each other, and I can tell you if any of your *friends* come around here to cause trouble, they'll meet a wall of resistance a mile high."

"So everything is perfect in la-la land."

Brian had to stop a chuckle—Rocklin sounded ridiculous. "No, it isn't perfect. But this isn't la-la land either. It is as close to heaven as I can imagine. The men know about me and David. We share a room in the bunkhouse."

Rocklin's mouth dropped open.

"Yeah. We care about each other. Hell, David loved me enough to bring you here so I could get some sort of closure." Brian took another step closer. "By the way, just so you know, the Wagoners know what the men did to me. They know I was set up, and from what I hear, they aren't happy about it. So you might think real hard about throwing your lot in with those men. Come spring, they might just find themselves on the outside looking in." Brian stared at Rocklin. "You don't have to live your life like this. You can have more and be happy." He knew his words had fallen on deaf ears. "No one from here will say anything to anyone at the Flying C. If you want to keep who you are a secret, then we won't betray that."

Brian looked toward the door and then back at Rocklin. He waited for him to get the hint and then glanced at David, wondering why Rocklin wasn't leaving.

"I met him in town and drove him out," David said.

"I overheard you guys talking, and I'll take him back if you like," Haven offered as he came into the room. He was the boss, and it was his house, after all. "I have to make a run into town anyway." It was clear from Haven's tone that he didn't have much use for Rocklin. Haven got his coat and motioned toward the door.

As Rocklin passed by, Brian stopped him with a touch on his arm. Rocklin turned to him with a scowl, and Brian pulled his hand away and shook his head. Nothing he could say or do would make one bit of difference. Brian had gotten what he needed, and that would have to be the end of it. Brian stepped back and looked on as Haven left the house with Rocklin behind him. Brian walked over to the window and watched as they made their way across the yard. He could almost see Rocklin returning to the person he'd known back at the Flying C, and by the time he reached Haven's truck, his usual swagger had started to make an appearance.

Brian turned away from the window. "I hope Haven's going to be okay."

Phillip chuckled as he came in from the kitchen. "I hope Rocklin is going to be okay. More than once I had to stop Haven from coming in here to beat the crap out of him. Maybe if we're lucky, Rocklin will keep his mouth shut and get back where he's supposed to be."

"Let's hope so." Brian nodded. "I appreciate you letting us use your living room for that little talk." He extended his hand, and David took it. "We should get back to the bunkhouse so we can leave you in peace." He put on his outerwear and got ready to go.

Phillip saw them to the door, and they stepped out into the floodlit yard. They walked over to the bunkhouse, but David stopped him before they got there and led him around the barn and then out farther to a small rise just off the road. They climbed to the top. It wasn't very high, but it had a great view of the surrounding land. Almost everything was still covered in white. In places, where the cattle had tamped down the snow, there were darker patches, but mostly the land looked clean, if a little stark, especially in the near darkness. "It's going to be cold tonight," Brian observed and glanced up at the sky, which was rapidly filling with stars.

"I'll keep you warm." David moved closer, settling behind him and wrapping his arms around Brian's chest. Brian leaned back into the embrace and closed his eyes. The air was bracing as the chill settled in, but he was warm next to David. "Did you get what you needed?"

"I think so. It's over, me and Rocklin. Not that there was ever anything serious between us. It's nice to know where you stand, and now I know."

"You tried to help him." David tugged him a little tighter as the cold breeze blew around them.

"What else could I do? He needed to hear what I had to say. It fell on deaf ears, though, and he's going to do what he wants to do because he doesn't see himself as gay. But I tried, and I feel pretty good for making the effort. Rocklin isn't a bad guy, but he's mired in fear. I think we've all been there—it's just that I doubt he'll ever come out of it." Brian grew quiet. He didn't want to talk about Rocklin or the Flying C. It was just the two of them and the land, wind, and stars. Brian reached up and pulled his hat down a little lower on his head.

"That's part of why I love you. You have a good heart. It would have been easy for you to write Rocklin off completely, but instead you gave him a chance. And who knows? He may think about what you said, and it may help him."

Brian began to laugh. "I'm sorry. But it's more likely that I wasted my breath. Rocklin isn't a smart man. His vision of himself is wrapped up in how the people around him see him. That isn't going to change. He needs approval, and as long as he's surrounded by people like those men at the Flying C, he'll remain the way he is." Brian shrugged. "Not that it matters any longer. I don't intend to see him or any of the people there again. I have a home, and someone who loves me." Brian turned in David's arms and locked onto his gaze. "And someone I love. That's all that matters."

David tilted his head to the side and parted his lips. Brian moved in, and David pulled him closer, eliminating any remaining space between them. Their lips met in flashes of light that rivaled the stars above. Not that Brian could see them. His eyes were closed, and every ounce of his being centered on David's lips caressing his.

"We could take this inside," David said.

Brian nodded, but didn't move away. He wanted this moment to last. Eventually, David took his hand, and they descended the rise and slowly walked back toward the bunkhouse. They passed some of the other men on their way, but said nothing. They were lost in their own world, and for now, that was where they wanted to be.

Inside, Gus had made dinner, and they sat at the table, side by side, their legs touching. They ate without offering a great deal to the conversation, but no one seemed to mind. When they were done, Brian helped clean up, and then he and David said good night, walked down the hallway to Brian's room, and closed the door.

The room felt like a sanctuary. The guys knew why they were in there and no one would disturb them. It was their private time, and the world outside wouldn't intrude on them for the next few hours. Brian stood at the end of the bed and looked at David with new eyes. He loved him, and as soon as he'd said the words, his last reservations had fallen away. It was like putting the last piece in a two-thousand-piece jigsaw puzzle. The picture was complete—everything fit and it was perfect.

David leaned against the closed door, and Brian slowly moved toward him. Without a word, he began unbuttoning David's shirt. David drew him close, kissing him with so much energy Brian couldn't make his fingers work. He simply stood there and returned David's kiss.

He got David's shirt open eventually and pushed it down his shoulders. David shrugged it off, and Brian managed to get his off as well. Then he tugged his undershirt up over his head and shivered slightly as David ran his warm hands along his side and over to his chest. He dropped the shirt, and David wrapped his arms around Brian's back to tug him closer. David licked his chest, breathing heavily against him. "I love how you smell. It's you mixed with the ranch and the land. All of it is there each time I breathe." He sucked at Brian's nipple, and Brian stretched, his legs shaking with excitement.

Brian moved slowly toward the bed. He thought he might fall, but David held him tight. The mattress touched the back of his legs, and David pressed him back and down, guiding him onto the bed and then making sure he was comfortable.

Brian kicked off his shoes, and David did the same before climbing on the bed. Then Brian was engulfed in strong arms and returned each and every kiss, measure for measure. Brian chuckled as David licked his way down his side. Brian scooted away. "That tickles."

"Well, we don't want that." David shifted and lightly sucked at the base of his neck. That brought a completely different sensation, and the giggles subsided in favor of a small moan.

"How do you do that?" Brian whispered.

"What, find those spots you like?"

Brian nodded.

"It's part of the fun." David grinned. "I bet some of the ones I've found you didn't even know about. Like this...." David licked just above his hip. Brian whimpered and tried to move away, but David held him still, increasing the sensation.

"God," Brian groaned. He hadn't even gotten his pants off and he was about two seconds from coming. David backed off and went to work on his belt and jeans, tugging them off and then whirling them over his head like a lasso before dropping them to the floor. "Come on."

"Hey, I got you out of your pants. That's always something to celebrate."

Brian had no intention of arguing, and when David gently rubbed the bulge in his shorts, he forgot about everything else. He clamped his eyes closed and rode the waves of pleasure. "Touch me," he whimpered.

David stopped. "I'll do a lot more than that."

Brian quivered, and David slowly ran his warm hands up his thighs, cupping his balls gently. He held his breath and wished he could simply will the last of his clothes away. When David slipped his fingers beneath the band of his briefs and tugged them down, he sighed with anticipation.

David's hot breath sizzled on his cock, but he didn't touch him, just warmed him, and then, with the lightest touch, David licked up his length. Brian's breath hitched and he swallowed hard. Damn, that felt good, but he needed more. Brian thrust his hips forward, and David took the hint and sucked Brian into his mouth, slowly sliding his lips down his length. "Damn."

David took him deeper, humming softly as he sucked. Brian wasn't going to last long. David had him so keyed up he was already balancing on the knife's edge. Then David backed away, and Brian gasped for air. He didn't want to come, not yet. It was way too soon. Brian closed his eyes and breathed as calmly as he could. He felt David slowly moving around him and then his weight settled on top of him and David kissed him. Brian wound his arms and legs around David and they held still, just the two of them lying together, nothing between them, everything open.

"No more secrets," Brian whispered between kisses.

"Okay," David returned.

They held each other for a long time. Brian didn't want to let go, and it seemed David didn't either. When David finally entered him, slow and thick, he kissed away Brian's gasp and sighs. They were connected now, together as one. When David moved, so did Brian. What amazed him, no matter how many times they were together, was how David listened to him. He didn't even have to say anything and David knew what he wanted. He read the smallest signs and acted just the way Brian needed. Sometimes he didn't know what he wanted, but David did. He left Brian breathless, wanting more, and then gave it to him. David opened himself up and gave time and time again, to Brian's unrivaled delight. He never knew things with another person could be so good or feel so right. They never had in the past, but alone in his room with David, everything felt as it should. He had all he wanted and more.

"That's it," David whispered into Brian's ear. "Touch yourself. I want to watch you and feel you. I want you to know that it's only me and it's only you. There won't be anyone else for as long as you want me."

"David," Brian breathed as his mind began to cloud with desire. He couldn't think and he couldn't speak. All he could do was look into David's eyes to keep the entire world from flying apart into millions of little pieces. Passion and desire built and built, David pushing him higher and higher, giving him everything except the last little bit he needed. That he held back again and again, until Brian begged for it. He could take no more.

He didn't know which way to turn, until he held David to him and said, "Please."

David sped up and Brian moved with each thrust. He needed to come so badly. It was all he could think about. Nothing else mattered except being with David and finally tumbling over the abyss. When he went, it was like nothing else ever. He flew and David was right there with him.

A HALF hour later, once they'd both been able to clean up, Brian lay on his back, staring up at the old ceiling. "What are you staring at so intently?" David asked in the darkness.

"Nothing." He shifted and sighed. "Did you ever dream of having your own place? I used to. My dad worked and managed a spread for someone else his whole life. I know he dreamed of having his own ranch, but he never got it before he died. He had a family to support and was never able to save up the money."

"I thought about it. But it's real hard. Used to be a guy could save up and buy a place. Now they're all too expensive. The price of land is so high it isn't something a guy can save up to buy. Dakota inherited his portion of the ranch, and so did Haven. They were born here and they'll live here their entire lives. It isn't likely they'll have kids to leave it to, but who knows. I knew Dakota's father, and he was something else. I never knew Haven's dad, and from all accounts he was a piece of work, but he passed this portion of the ranch on to Haven. I suppose if they decided to sell, a big company would buy them out."

"I guess it's just one of those things you dream of," Brian said.

"Hey. Dream big and often." David tugged him a little closer. "There's nothing wrong with having a dream."

Brian didn't answer. "Part of my dream came true, anyway. Whenever I pictured myself on my ranch, I always had someone to share it with."

"You already have that, and it doesn't matter whether we're here or on our own place. We both have someone to share it with." David rolled over and pulled Brian close. "I'm here and I'm not going anywhere."

"But what if things change, like they did for you and Mario?" Brian asked, finally putting words to his last fear.

"Then we'll talk about it. I don't want anything like that to happen again. So we'll talk." David kissed him lightly. "And we'll share things with each other. Love isn't a sprint—it's a marathon. It takes place over years, not weeks, and you have to work at it all the time. I didn't with Mario. I don't think either of us did. We figured things would just work out, but they didn't. Not on their own."

"Yeah."

"I can't give you any guarantees. All I have to give you is my word. I love you and I'll do everything I can to make sure you're happy." David brushed the hair out of his eyes. "I love that your hair is starting to curl. It reminds me of when I first saw you all those years ago. I liked you then, but I love you now." David kissed him hard, and the last of Brian's doubts melted away. This was what he'd wanted, and now he had it. Brian closed his eyes and returned the kiss with everything he had.

Epilogue

OLD MAN Winter hung on as long and as tight as he could. But finally, spring arrived. Thankfully for everyone in the area, winter didn't give up the ghost all at once. It died slowly, so the snow and ice melted gradually over time instead of in a single flooding rush. Brian knew no one was more grateful for that than Haven, who fussed and worried whenever the temperature got too high. The good thing was that the land was well hydrated and the drinking holes full. In that way, it had been a good winter, the heavy snowfall replenishing the aquifers. It had also refilled the ponds and other water sources for the ranch.

Brian leaned against one of the paddock fences, admiring the horse and her young colt inside. He walked slowly on still wobbly legs while his mama waited for him to return. She called to him, and he hurried back over and began to eat. The little thing had a healthy appetite.

David came up from behind him and took the place next to him against the fence. "They look like they're doing fine."

"They are. It's some sort of miracle they're both still with us."

"The miracle was you and Wally working together to deliver him. You two never gave up on either of them." David rested his arm around Brian's shoulder. "I've seen plenty of equine births, and I've even helped with a few, but I've never seen one like that. And how Wally managed to save both the mother and colt is beyond belief."

"He doesn't give up, and neither do I. They were both strong." They'd had to help in the birth a lot more than they should have, and David was right, they should have lost at least one of them, but they hadn't. Mama and colt were standing together in paddock-surrounded bliss. "I chalk it up to the wonders of spring and let it go at that."

David chortled. "You've been saying that about everything for the past week."

"Well, it's true. It was one hell of a winter, and other than how everything ended up, I don't want to go through another one like that ever again." Brian wriggled his fingers in front of his face. Both he and David were lucky they had all their fingers and toes. Hell, Brian knew he was lucky to be alive. "So what do you have planned for this glorious Sunday? The stalls are clean and the horses are all enjoying the spring air."

"Well...." David turned toward him. "I thought we'd go for a ride." David backed away from the fence and walked toward the barn. Brian watched him go, admiring the ass encased in those tight jeans. To think that butt was his, along with the rest of the amazing man it was attached to. The thought brought a grin to Brian's face. David stopped and turned around. "Are you going to stand there ogling or help me get ready?"

Brian didn't move and David lifted his hands to rest them on his hips.

"I'm thinking, okay? Ogling seems like the smart thing from my point of view." He took a few steps closer. "How about you get the horses ready, and I'll watch?"

David flipped him the finger, and Brian laughed and walked toward the barn. It had seemed like a really good idea to him.

Inside, he got Mazy brushed and saddled, then led her out into the yard. David came right behind him. Brian got the idea that the ogling was happening in the other direction. He glanced over his shoulder and smiled. Yup, David had that faraway, lustful look he got whenever Brian caught him leering. Not that he minded at all. Hell, he hoped when they were eighty and sitting on the porch in their rocking chairs, David still got that look when it was Brian's turn to get the ice tea.

"So where are we riding to?"

"We're just taking a ride."

Brian knew that was a lie, but he'd let David have his bit of mystery. If David had something planned, he didn't want to spoil the surprise.

He mounted his horse, and David did the same. Brian knew he could be mean and try to take the lead to force David's hand, but he hung back and followed David out across the range. Besides, the view was much better from the back.

"You know you're supposed to be watching where you're going, right?" David said at one point.

Brian chuckled. "I am. I'm following you and letting your butt point the way." He couldn't see it, but he knew David had rolled his eyes after he turned around to face forward. It was amazing to have someone to tease and joke with, someone who was his and understood him. For the longest time, his sense of humor had been kept on ice. He hadn't joked with or teased anyone because of the possible repercussions. Also, since he'd been keeping a secret, he hadn't wanted to draw attention to himself. Now a new freedom had bloomed inside of him, and he saw the same things in David. Things that used to bother them didn't any longer. Being happy was a wonderful thing.

The land around them was still waking from winter's long slumber, but spring was definitely in full swing. The grasses had greened up, and the limbs on the trees were getting thicker as the buds began to open. Soon everything would be lush and green. It was all just on the cusp. "Are we heading over to Dakota and Wally's?"

"As a start," David answered. They followed the trail and arrived at the yard. David dismounted, and Brian did the same. They tethered their horses, and Wally came out of the house.

"I take it you're here to see our latest additions?" Wally smiled. "They're just around back."

Brian looked at David, who winked at him. Then they followed Wally around the house and out to a single pen away from the others. "Now, be quiet and don't make any sudden moves. She's been pretty quiet, but we don't want to scare her."

Brian looked at David again, and he grinned. They approached the pen, where a tigress lay on her side. She yawned and then lifted her head warily as they approached. Brian heard a soft growl from her throat.

"It's okay," Wally said softly, making her listen for him. It was the same trick Brian used with horses. Make them strain to hear. It forced them to concentrate on something other than their fear. "No one is going to hurt you or try to take your cubs."

They stopped. Sure enough, after a few seconds, she moved her protective paw, and Brian saw two cubs nursing. They were adorable as they struggled to get closer for more milk. "Did you know she was pregnant?"

"Not until a few days before she gave birth. I could never get close enough, and from what I was told when I got her from the circus, she was old and they were simply looking for a place where she could retire. Apparently someone left her and the male together and... well, nature has her own way and does things in her own time."

"What will you do with them when they get older?"

Wally turned to them and smiled. "I have zoos lining up to take all three of them. My goal is usually to find them homes, but

Marta here is a very rare cat. In the wild, much of her habitat is gone, so there aren't many left. She's a Bengal, and without captive breeding programs, they will become extinct. The fact that she has cubs already means I'll get enough for the three of them to keep the rescue going for six months."

"She's beautiful," Brian said.

"And deadly," David added.

"Very, especially now that she's had her cubs." Wally slowly backed away. Brian and David did the same. Then they headed back around the side of the house.

"I still can't get over how you can do this. I mean, I know you love animals, but these aren't the petting, cuddly kind."

Wally chuckled. "I know. But it has its rewards. Marta's owners had given up on her just a month or so ago. Now she'll be helping to save her entire species from extinction. I'd say that's a pretty good reward."

Brian couldn't argue with that. "I noticed some empty cages."

"Yeah. I lost a few over the winter. They were old, and the cold got to be too much. It was their time, and they died peacefully. That's all any of us can ask." Wally turned toward the house and went inside without saying more.

Brian had come to learn that was Wally's way. Even when there was nothing he could do, he took each animal's care very seriously. Brian wished he'd kept his mouth shut.

"Let's go," David whispered. He led Brian over to the horses. They mounted and headed back toward home. At about halfway, David veered off and took them out across the acreage. Brian knew there was an old service road back here somewhere, and he wondered if that was where David was heading. David slowed and turned along the old gravel road, and Brian did the same. They followed it for a little while until they began to climb.

The horses made it easily, and David guided his horse onto a clearing that looked just big enough for a car or truck.

David dismounted and held his reins. Brian followed suit. David looked around and found a place to tie the horses. Once they were secured, he led Brian to the top of the small hill. "I used to come here with Mario sometimes. At night you can see the lights from the house, and the stars seem so close you swear you can reach out and touch them." David tugged him closer. Brian's hat fell to the ground, but he left it there as David pulled him into a kiss.

David wrapped his arms around Brian's waist, ensuring that they were as close together as possible.

"Is this why you brought me here? To make out?" Brian asked.

David smiled. "Can you think of a better idea?" David didn't wait for an answer. He simply kissed him again, and all other thoughts flew from Brian's mind. "I didn't think so," David added breathlessly when they came up for air.

"So is this the official ranch make-out spot?"

"From what I understand," David said and then gently guided Brian down onto the grass.

Brian wondered if this was maybe a little much, but as soon as David kissed him again, the protest died on his lips.

They made enthusiastic love in the spring sunshine. Unlike when they were in the bunkhouse, they cried and yelled their passion out over the land, rejoicing in what they had and what they'd found together. Brian clung to David as they moved together, connected body and soul. This was it for him. Brian knew he had found the one person in the world for him.

Climbing the heights of passion together, bare-assed—hell, bare-everythinged—open to the sun and the warm spring air, Brian alternated between looking at David and at the crystal blue sky overhead. He owed so much to whoever or whatever saw to it that things worked out for the best. He'd never been a religious man, but as he got closer and closer to the climax of his life, Brian swore he saw the face of God. For an instant, he wondered what he should ask for. He closed his eyes and held on for dear life as David pushed them that last little distance, and then they tumbled into the abyss of happiness that went on and on.

When Brian came back to himself, the warm breeze caressed him, the sun shone around him, and David held him tightly. He had everything he could possibly want. Amen.

ANDREW GREY grew up in western Michigan with a father who loved to tell stories and a mother who loved to read them. Since then he has lived all over the country and traveled throughout the world. He has a master's degree from the University of Wisconsin-Milwaukee and now works full time on his writing. Andrew's hobbies include collecting antiques, gardening, and leaving his dirty dishes anywhere but in the sink (particularly when writing). He considers himself blessed with an accepting family, fantastic friends, and the world's most supportive and loving husband. Andrew currently lives in beautiful historic Carlisle, Pennsylvania.

Visit Andrew's website at http://www.andrewgreybooks.com and blog at http://andrewgreybooks.livejournal.com/.
E-mail him at andrewgrey@comcast.net.

Previously in Stories from the Range!

A Volatile Range

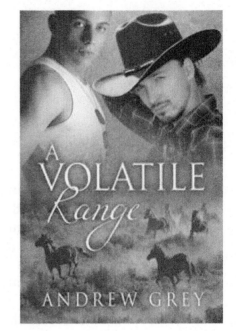

Stories from the Range:
Book 6

By Andrew Grey

Since mustering out of the Marines, Gordon Fisher has been off the grid and out of money, so when a group of ecoterrorists promises him big bucks to set some mistreated animals free, Gordon agrees. Unfortunately, the animals are Wally Schumacher's large cats, and one of them decides to take a chunk out of Gordon.

Still hurting from a breakup, Mario Laria finds Gordon and escorts him back to Dakota's ranch at gunpoint, only to have his heartstrings tugged on when he discovers Gordon is living out of his truck.

With Dakota doctoring, Wally wanting Gordon gone for good, and Mario falling in love, Gordon hangs on for the ride. But what looms on his horizon threatens to tear apart what little hope he's found. No one knows Gordon's past keeps him up at night, and the military wants answers he just can't give.

Other books in the Range Series

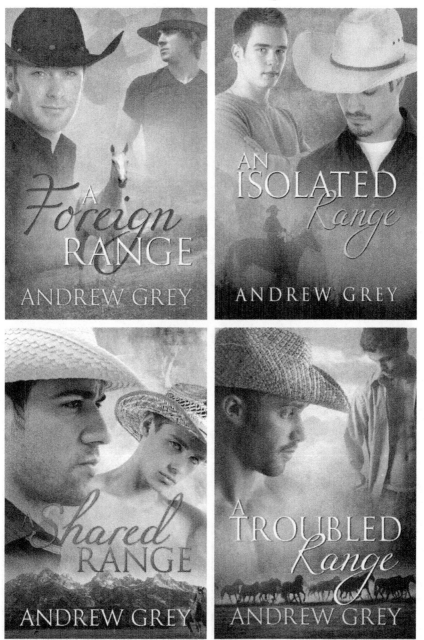

Good Fight Series

THE GOOD FIGHT — ANDREW GREY

THE FIGHT WITHIN — ANDREW GREY

ANDREW GREY — TAKODA AND HORSE

THE FIGHT FOR IDENTITY — ANDREW GREY

http://www.dreamspinnerpress.com

The Senses Series

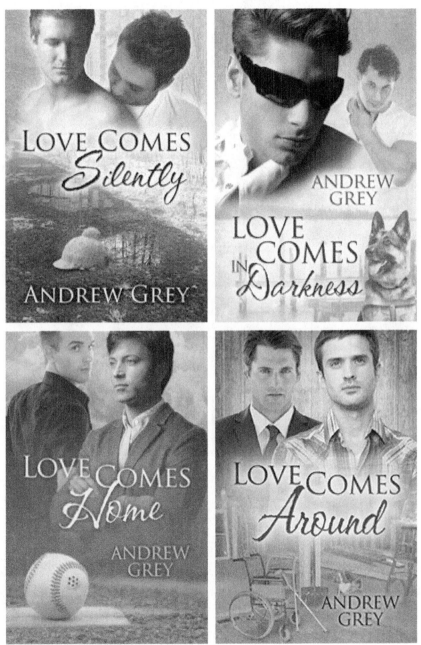

http://www.dreamspinnerpress.com

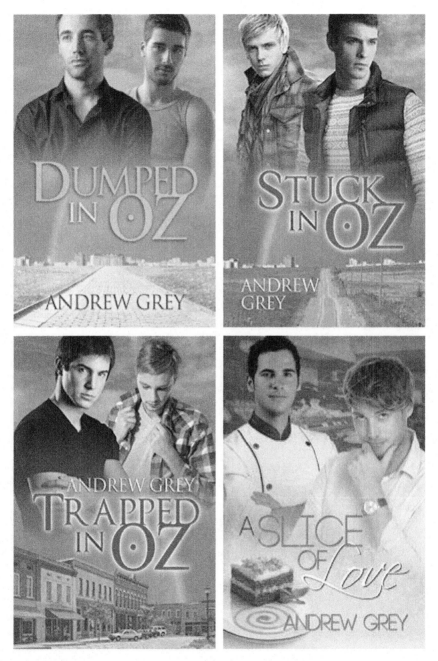

http://www.dreamspinnerpress.com

http://www.dreamspinnerpress.com

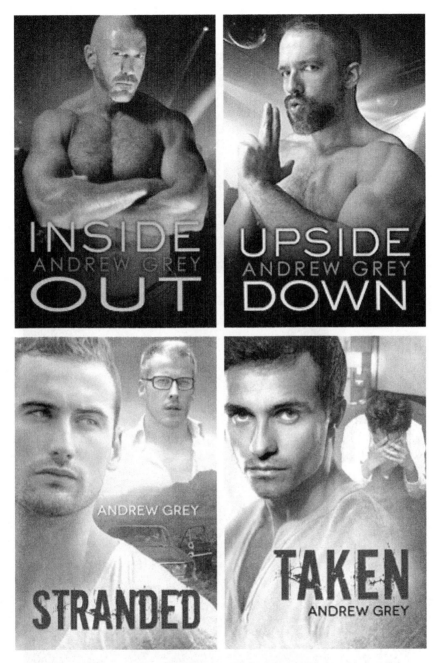

http://www.dreamspinnerpress.com

CPSIA information can be obtained at www.ICGtesting.com
Printed in the USA
BVOW06s1553230815

414613BV00010B/219/P